DC SUMNER

Storm of War

First edition

ISBN: 979-8-9901581-8-4

*This book was professionally typeset on Reedsy.
Find out more at reedsy.com*

Contents

Dedication

To my girls, for always dealing with my shenanigans. I love you all more than anything, and I wouldn't be able to do this without you.

Prologue

The power of fire at his fingertips, and yet, he was cold. So cold. Hands broken beyond use that only time would be able to mend. Augustus shivered, either from the freezing ground he sat on or the bitter cold feeling of regret that rippled through his body.

Why? he thought. *Why did I allow myself to become this? Why did things have to turn out this way?*

He knew he was only getting what he deserved. And now the beast stalks back into the prison that holds the man, a devilish smile glinting in the pale darkness. "Why so glum, Augustus?" Aros asks.

Augustus turned his eyes away, choosing to not answer. The shadows gripped his head, and forced him to look back at his master. "I asked you a question."

"How long will you hold me?" the man asked. "Please, just kill me. End my suffering."

"Begging?" Aros prodded. "Really, Augustus, I thought that would be beneath you. I will not be letting you go anytime soon, my dear." Augustus' face fell. "You and I have gone through far too much for me to just allow you to leave now. No, I will hold onto you until the very end."

A single tear slipped down Augustus' cheek. "I promise, I won't tell them anything. I won't even go back to Asmaria. Just let me go." He pled with all the desperation he could muster, but it wasn't enough.

"No, I think not," he replied. "Much too risky. Besides, how else will I force you to watch me peel the flesh from your brat's bones?"

Anger replaced the sadness and despair he was feeling. The rage built, and despite his crooked fingers, flames danced along their tips. "I will escape from this place! I will see to it that you are permanently removed from this world and I will dance upon your grave!" he bellowed as the Demon King sauntered away, laughing.

Aros willed the shadows to carry him up from the pit that held Augustus and they obeyed. Roughly 50 feet deep, the man had yet to figure out a way to escape. He also hadn't tried very hard. The pain in his hands was minimal as long as he sat still. It would seem that Aros intended to keep him alive, but just barely. Once a week food scraps were tossed down the pit.

Not much of what he was given was edible, and now, flies and rotten stench filled the air around the chamber.

"I have to get out of here," Augustus mumbled to himself.

He steeled his nerves, grasping a finger with the opposite palm. Slowly, he pulled on the broken appendage. He grunted and gasped as the joints and bones popped.

The searing pain was enough to bring tears to his eyes again as he grabbed another finger. They wouldn't heal perfectly but it would be better than leaving them at the odd angles in which they lay. After getting them as straight as possible, his mind began working to formulate an escape plan.

Awake

sh tried standing again but his legs were not being cooperative. The doctor helped him back up and into the bed.

"You have to take it easy," she told him. "You've been in a coma for around a year."

He couldn't believe it.

"Here, eat this. It'll help." She handed him some heala.

Ash took it gratefully and popped the small morsel into his mouth. Warmth spread through him. "Thank you," he rasped, his throat still feeling mangled.

"You should know," the doctor began, "I've alerted the Guardians of your awakening."

He sighed, "That's alright. It's time I pay for the things I've done." The doctor nodded solemnly, and left him to his thoughts.

Raimir, he reached out to the giant falcon. *Where are you?*

I'm in my realm. I've just become strong enough again to hear your voice.

Ash smiled; it was good to hear from his friend again. *I suspect the Guardians will be here any second. I don't know what's going to happen, but I do know that I'll be punished. I deserve to be.*

Don't be so hard on yourself, Raimir said. *Mistakes are what bring forth growth, so long as you don't let them consume you.*

Ash chuckled, *You're too smart, you know that? When can I see you?*

A moment passed that was so long, Ash wasn't sure Raimir was still listening. Then, *I think it would be best for you to regain your strength before I return. If your body is too weak for the training you shall endure, you will die.*

A jolt went through him. *Training? What are you talking about?*

Don't dwell on any of that for now. Just focus on getting your mind and body stronger. Deal with the Guardians and your friends. I will come to you when the time is right.

Okay, was all Ash could squeeze out. He was disappointed. The relief that Raimir was alive is what had woken him up. Ash was disheartened at knowing he'd have to wait to see the colossal bird.

Shouts in the hallway alerted Ash; his head snapped to the door as the four Guardians burst in. They were arguing with the doctor fervently. Ash cowered in his bed. Magical essence swirled around the Guardians. It was clear that they were still upset with him.

"I know you're the Guardians but he is *my* patient," the doctor yelled. "So stop with the magic before you ruin my hospital!" The magic dissipated as they all took a few calming breaths. The doctor stepped aside.

Ash was assaulted by questions that came from the Guardians but it was too much to make out. It was making his head hurt. He slapped his hands over his ears and shook his head until they stopped.

"I can't understand all of you at the same time."

"Fair enough," Bora said, then cleared her throat. When she spoke, the volume was so great that Ash thought it would burst his eardrums. "WHAT WERE YOU THINKING?"

A knot was forming in his throat. "I'm sorry," he choked out.

Avani put his hand on Bora's shoulder as they bobbed up and down. She was very angry with him. "Ash, I need you to understand the severity of what you've done. You attacked us and as the leaders of Asmaria, we cannot allow that to go unpunished. Your actions got someone killed."

The tears hit him hard. They spilled down his face and he couldn't stop them from coming. He wiped at his face, choking out between sobs, "I know. . . I'm so sorry. I didn't. . . mean for this. . . to happen." To them a year had passed, but to Ash it was just yesterday that he saw Aros take Draven's life.

"Whatever punishment you come up with," Ash said, "I'll gladly accept. Just know that nothing you do to me will ever replace the guilt that I have." His head hung low. He meant the things he'd said.

A man dressed in the orange of the fire Guardian stepped forward. He was a short, umber-skinned man. He reached his hand forward and Ash clasped his fingers around the man's forearm. "My name is Dihren. I can see that you feel deep remorse for the things you've done, however, my colleagues are correct. Your behavior must be corrected, not because you are wicked, but because we must have order."

Their handshake broke as Ash nodded. "I understand, believe me."

The Guardians seemed to release a collective breath. Leena said, "Well, good then. We assumed you would have put up more of a fight. However, since you are in agreement with us things will go much smoother. We shall convene on your behalf once you've made a full recovery. Deal?"

He smiled, "Deal."

"Did you hear?" Kane asked.

"You'll need to be a tad more specific," Quinn said.

Neither of them had been in the mood for smiles or jokes as of late, however, Kane couldn't help himself when he told her, "Ash is awake."

She didn't—couldn't—form a response. Quinn turned and sprinted as fast as her legs would carry her. It wasn't fast enough. She whipped her hands in front of her, conjuring a wave and then freezing it. It was effortless to glide across the ice toward the hospital. Quinn was sure to melt it with a flourish of her arm as she approached the doors, Kane landing softly beside her.

He shook his head as she looked at him. "I knew you couldn't wait."

A year had gone by since she'd spoken to Ash. All three of them had birthdays come and go. She didn't feel like celebrating at all in that time. The last time she had spoken to Ash, it hadn't gone well.

"What if he's still mad at me?" she asked him.

"Well, he's definitely had enough time to sleep it off."

She glared at him. "I'm serious."

He sighed, "If he's still mad, then there is something wrong with him. After what he did he's lucky we're even visiting him."

That statement had some truth to it. They'd lost a valuable ally in the battle against Aros just because they got ahead of themselves. Ash could have stopped Draven from going. Quinn half blamed herself for hurting him. Had she not rejected him, Ash probably wouldn't have run off halfcocked.

Kane opened the door for her and she slowly walked in. Ash laid in his bed staring out of a window. His hair was shaggier than she remembered it. It had been a few months since she last visited him in the infirmary. His body had lost some of the muscle tone, but not much, thanks to the heala being fed to him.

"Hello," was all she could utter. His head slowly turned. Quinn's fingers twiddled with each other.

A wide smile stretched across his face. "Hello," he repeated.

Kane marched in front of where she was frozen and threw his arms around Ash. "Geez, you could use a bath." Kane was already back to his teasing, pinching his nose. Ash punched him on the arm playfully.

The two boys looked at her until she noticed and crossed the room. "Is it okay if I hug you?" she asked.

Ash chuckled, "Of course." And she did. She began crying into his shoulder.

He pulled her away as the sobs softened, holding her face in his hands. "Why are you crying?"

"I'm not sure," she admitted. "I guess I've just missed you *so* much. And I didn't know if you'd be happy to see me. I didn't know if you'd even wake up."

"Why wouldn't I be—," it seemed that he remembered the rejection. "Oh. Yeah. Look, I've been out of it so long that I don't even really care about all that anymore."

"Oh," she replied. How could he not care? Her cheeks burned.

"Yeah, I just want things to go back to halfway normal, you

know? I'm ready to get back to training. Gotta catch back up to this dork." He shoved his finger toward Kane.

Kane laughed. "Catch back up? Dude, you were never *close* to my level."

They began fake wrestling in his bed, laughing with each other.

"Okay, well, it was nice seeing you, Ash. I'm glad you're awake," she said as she turned to leave.

"Hey," he called after her. She turned to see Kane being held in a headlock. "Thanks for visiting me. I'll see you soon?"

Quinn smiled, saying, "Yeah. See you soon."

Reasoning of The Father

Rick's beard seemed to have doubled in length from what Ash remembered. His adoptive father held him close as they shuffled down the hallway. Ash wanted to get back out there. His legs weren't carrying him very fast and he still felt weak, but leaning on Rick made things easier.

"I wasn't sure if you were ever going to come back to us," Rick told him.

Ash chuckled nervously, "Yeah, I wasn't sure if I was going to either. I just kind of gave up."

"Why?"

He sighed. "I've done nothing but let everyone down. It seems like failure is all I'm good at."

Rick stopped, grabbing Ash by the shoulders. "Are you kidding me? You're so strong, Ash. Much stronger than I could *ever* be."

Ash couldn't hold back his smile. "Oh, don't say that. I learned from the best." Rick hugged him close and then they continued through the doors to outside.

The sun was bright; Ash squinted, breathing in the sea-salty air. "I have to admit it's nice to be awake again."

"What kept you from coming back sooner?"

Ash thought about it for a moment. "To me, it's as if everything that I did *just* happened. I forced my mind into a chasm of darkness because the pain of living with myself was too much to bear. I thought I had gotten both Draven and Raimir killed; I kept calling out to him but he wouldn't answer. Then, he finally did. Raimir's voice snapped me awake."

"Listen, guilt is a powerful emotion," Rick said. "To deal with guilt, I say it's best to face the consequences of your actions. If you're remorseful show it and, with time, you'll heal."

"Thanks, Rick," Ash said.

The seasoned man smiled. "Let's get you home."

"Wow," Ash marveled, "you've been a little busy."

Rick laughed, rubbing the back of his neck. "Yeah, I've spent a large portion of my time learning as much as I could about Asmaria's history. I was hoping that at some point I would find something that will help us get rid of Aros for good, but so far I haven't found anything."

Tomes were piled and scattered all over the little hovel that the two of them called home.

Ash's legs were feeling a bit better already, and he walked around the hut on his own. He plopped down on the couch and let out a sigh. "I'm glad to be back. I can't wait to get back to training."

"Take it easy," Rick said. "You've still got the trial to get through first."

Ash let out a groan. Why did Rick have to remind him?

"I guess I kind of forgot about that for a second there," he admitted.

"I obviously can't protect you," Rick said, attempting to tidy up the place some. "I don't have any sort of pull with the Guardians; they trust me enough to treat me like an ordinary citizen now, which I'm grateful for, but that's about it. However, I will be by your side through it all no matter what."

Ash smiled. "I know. You've always been there. From the very beginning you've had my back. Even after what I did to you."

Ash's eyes found his feet. More guilt. The scene flashed in his mind as if it were yesterday when he almost killed Rick. His power to wield lightning showed in a fit of anger when Ash lashed out at the man, striking him and sending him flying through their apartment window.

Rick rubbed his chest, seeming to remember the moment as well. "Ash, you don't have to worry about that. I've moved on. I've forgiven you. Now, forgive yourself."

"Right," Ash said. "I think I'm going to turn in. Big day tomorrow. Goodnight."

"Goodnight, son."

Ash knew he would struggle to fall asleep, and if he did it would be riddled with bad dreams. The following day he would stand trial for his crimes. He had no clue how it would go and he admitted—if only to himself—that he was scared. Terrified even. All he could do was hope that the punishment wouldn't be too harsh. Defeating Aros was still at the top of his to-do list, and he would need to get stronger if that was going to happen.

Sentencing

Maybe it was the retreat into Ash's mind that gave him renewed courage to face his fears. He steeled himself as he and Rick walked through the doors to the Capitol building. The auditorium was filled with Asmarians. Ash looked for familiar faces, and found the Atlanteans to all be missing from the throng.

"You okay?" Rick asked, taking the seat next to him.

He nodded. "Yeah. I'm just ready to get all this over with."

Ash scanned the faces of the crowd, looking for any that may be friendly to him. He found Quinn and smiled at her which she returned. She was sitting next to Kane who was too busy speaking with Kailani to notice anything else.

"Silence, Asmarians," Avani's voice boomed, making Ash start. "Thank you all for your attendance. We are gathered for Ash's trial for the crime of disobeying direct orders given by the Guardians." He paused, letting the words linger.

In times past, trials were a more private affair. However, at some point within the last thousand years the tradition changed to allow the public to come watch trials unfold. The Guardians who created that rule found it to be effective at discouraging repeat offenses. Ash certainly hated having all the eyes watching him.

Ash stared at the crowd, willing his eyes not to drop to his feet.

"This disobedience directly caused an ally to lose his life," Avani continued. "As such, we cannot overlook it."

The group of mage leaders huddled together, whispering. When they parted Bora stepped forward. "How do you plead, guilty or not guilty?"

Ash stood, cleared his throat, and said definitively, "Guilty."

Bora's lips were pressed into a thin line as she nodded and stepped back. The Guardians went back to their huddle of whispers.

Leena addressed them all, "For these crimes, we find the accused guilty." Murmurs broke through the crowd. Ash didn't know—or care—what they were saying, however, his heart was racing to know what they were going to punish him with.

The water mage continued, "You will endure 100 hours of *grueling* community service." She smirked.

More murmurs arose from the onlookers. Perhaps they were unhappy with the punishment. Maybe many of them thought it wasn't severe enough.

Ash was relieved. He let loose a breath that he didn't know was being held.

Dihren finally broke his silence, "I'm assuming you're familiar with the term?"

"Yes, sir. Although, I'm curious what sort of tasks I will be doing?"

The Guardians smiled together and Dihren replied, "That is to be decided. If you accept this punishment, you will be bound by your word that you will complete any task that we assign. However, if you wish to appeal this decision, we can give you more information as to how that process works."

Ash waved his hands, "No, please. I accept. Graciously, might I add?"

"Very well," Avani said. He turned to the crowd. "Consider this matter resolved. You're all dismissed."

The mages dispersed and Ash approached the Guardians. "Hey, I just wanted to thank you guys. Also, I'm sorry for everything. I acted foolishly."

Avani crossed his arms. "Yes, you did. But it's behind us now. A year has passed and a lot has been happening. You have a lot to catch up on, which I'm sure your friends will be more than happy to assist you with. We have other matters to attend to." He gave a slight nod and turned away.

Ash found his friends with big smiles waiting on him as he turned around to leave. Rick put a hand on his shoulder and said, "Whew. Well, that's over with. It's time I get back to work."

Ash's brows furrowed. "Work?"

He chuckled, "Oh, right. I think it's best if I just show you."

Rick's workplace was a small building on the outskirts of the city. There were a couple of other Asmarians and Atlanteans inside. They were sitting around a large section of what looked like television screens.

"This," Rick said, spreading his arms wide, "is where we've been keeping tabs on Aros."

The screens weren't showing much; it looked like a news broadcast was playing from a European country. Ash couldn't even understand what was being said. Whichever city was being displayed had small fires burning throughout the streets.

He frowned. "I don't get it."

Rick began to explain, "The runes on the side of the screens are imbued with Atlantean magic which allows us to pick up on energy that Aros gives off. We haven't actually found him yet, but apparently he's been moving around all over the world. In some places, we find that graves have been upturned. In others, like this one, the people are going mad. His influence is everywhere and it's not good."

Kane jumped in, "It looks like he's simultaneously building an army and causing the people of the world to turn on each other."

"I see," Ash said. "So, what's the plan? I mean, why watch these screens? Are we actively trying to stop him?"

"That's kind of the issue," Quinn said. "We can't pinpoint his location. The scenes change so often and are so widely spread that we don't know how to find him. We've sent scouts to previous locations that have been affected by him, but of course he's never there. And there has yet to be any clues that would tell us where to look next."

"Wow," Ash shook his head. "So, you guys have just been sitting around watching screens while he runs rampant?"

"You're one to talk," Kailani jabbed.

"Excuse me?"

"You know nothing about what has been going on for the last year, and now that you're back you get to judge all of us? I don't think so!"

Ash felt his anger rise. He hadn't used magic in a year, but even so, he could see everyone's hair begin to rise with the static that wafted from him.

"Okay, let's all just calm down," Quinn interjected before things got out of hand.

Ash took a deep breath. "You're right," he told Kailani. "I'm sorry. I didn't mean any disrespect by it. I'm just… trying to acclimate to all this news."

She gave him a nod but didn't say anything further.

Rick cleared his throat. "Anyway, the Guardians have been allowing me to help monitor things here and help out with any of the tech issues that pop up. It's a little weird, I have to admit, seeing as this is part magic and technology. I enjoy it though."

The man looked happier than Ash ever remembered. He smiled.

"I'm glad they let you stay on Asmaria," he told him.

"Wake up." Ash woke with a start. Rick was standing in his doorway. "There's someone here to see you."

Ash had no idea of the time, but by the groggy feeling, he guessed it was still the middle of the night.

Avani waited on him outside their home. "Ready?" he asked as Ash stepped outside, rubbing the sleep from his eyes.

"Care to elaborate?"

Avani smiled. "It's time for your first community service task."

Ash groaned, "What time is it?"

Avani replied, "The sun should be up within the hour. And when it rises, you'll need to keep the worms at bay."

Ash stared at him, confused. "Worms? What are you talking about?"

"Come on, I'll show you."

Avani led him out of town and into the farmland where crops grew plentifully. The expanse of crops was hard to see in the dim torchlight. It consisted of all sorts of fruits and veggies that Ash could never remember the names of.

"This," Avani began, "will be your area of responsibility." It was a group of what looked like cabbages. The patch only had five rows of round veggies. Each row looked to be around twenty feet long.

"And you want me to do what?" Ash asked.

"Asmaria is home to a particularly annoying vegetarian worm species known as zygats. They like to surface as the sun dawns and steal these shurma plants. It's their favorite. Your job is to use that lightning of yours to zap the creatures before they can destroy everything. I doubt you destroy their entire nest, but they usually retreat after a couple of hours. This job is usually delegated to our fire mages, however, I thought it would be fitting to let you have the displeasure."

Ash scoffed. "Wow. Thanks. I feel honored."

Avani just laughed.

"You're enjoying this, aren't you?" Ash asked, looking at the man sideways.

"A little too much, I think," he admitted. "Any questions?"

"Yeah. How am I supposed to see them? Worms are usually tiny."

"Oh," Avani smiled, "you'll see these. Trust me."

"Okay," Ash sighed. "You *do* know I haven't wielded lightning in a year, right? How do you know that I can even still do it?"

"I don't. I guess we'll know after this though, won't we?"

Ash didn't answer. Avani walked off into the fading darkness. The earliest hint of light was beginning to creep over the horizon.

Burned Worms

vani was telling the truth when he told Ash he'd have no trouble seeing the zygats. The first one showed its ugly head if it could even be called that. Ash just assumed the head would pop up first but it was impossible to tell as both ends looked the same. The thing burst from the ground and wriggled towards the nearest shurma.

The length of its body was nearly the same as Ash's forearm and had to be at least three inches around. The tiniest of legs could be seen aiding the worm across the soil. The trail of mucus it left behind made Ash want to gag.

"Not today," he told the worm.

Ash began digging for the magic that flowed through him. The chunk of time Ash had missed made it difficult for him to find the magical energy. The giant worm was already chomping down on the verdant veggie and others were emerging.

There.

The amethyst lightning roared to life, blazing down his arms, and arcing between his fingertips. He took aim. In a flash, the purple lightning blasted from his hand and smote the zygat. Unfortunately, he was out of practice and burned the shurma to a crisp as well.

The worms were relentless; after destroying a few of the crops and all the zygats he could see, more appeared. After a couple of hours, however, the worms' ascension to the surface waned, and ultimately ceased.

Ash sat on a large rock near the crops, wiping the sweat from his brow. The work had exhausted him. It was going to take a while for his endurance to return.

After resting for a bit, he decided to jog back to his house. He couldn't. His body wasn't prepared for such exertion. About halfway there, his legs began to take on the likeness of jelly.

Ash sat on a wooden bench adjacent to the training field. Kane was leading the wind mages through an elaborate exercise. It almost looked like a fun sport. They were using gusts of wind to keep themselves afloat while simultaneously sending a spiked ball around at each other. If they messed up and allowed the thing to hit them, they'd surely regret it.

Kane floated around supervising effortlessly, no doubt thanks to the Rings of Sidhe—a gift from the Atlanteans that enhanced his wind magic tenfold.

The training session ended and Kane landed gently next to Ash on the bench.

"How's it going?" Kane asked.

"Well, I got my first task from the Guardians this morning. Worm zapper."

Kane laughed and said, "They got you taking care of the zygats? Nice!"

"I'm not sure 'nice' is the word I'd use," Ash said. "I didn't think it would be this hard to get back into the swing of things. I thought I was going to pass out before those stinking worms stopped coming."

"Well, just give it some time and I'm sure you'll be back to normal soon," Kane said reassuringly.

"So, are you like, leader of the wind mages now?"

"Something like that." Kane paused, considering what to say. "I'm not a Guardian by any means. That title still belongs to Bora. I am in charge of training all the others now, though. It's been fun, although, I wish it were under better circumstances." His expression turned grim.

"I can't help but think that all of this is my fault," Ash let the guilt take hold again.

"Why would you think that?"

Ash bounced his knees nervously. "If I had stopped Aros the first time our paths crossed, none of this would be happening."

"You need to let that go, Ash. No one is to blame for the evil Aros has committed except Aros. Even all that stuff with Draven. He was older than you. It's not totally your fault that he was able to persuade you to go with him. You were in a vulnerable state and he took advantage of it. Just let things go, man."

"Maybe you're right," he admitted.

Kane smiled and clapped him on the back. "Of course I am!" Kane stood up. "Now, let's go get some food. I'm starved!"

After they finished with lunch, Kane told Ash there was something he needed to see. He wouldn't say what it was, but that it was awesome, nonetheless.

They found themselves on one of Asmaria's beaches.

"What exactly are we waiting for?" Ash asked.

"Not what, but who," Kane responded, adding nothing more.

Ash poked around in the sand with a small stick, harassing

the tiny insects who lived there, when Kane said, "Finally."

Ash looked up and rose to his feet as the water began to ripple and a head of silvery hair emerged. Kailani waved at them.

"Ready?" she asked.

"Ready for what?" Ash asked in return.

"You haven't told him where we're going?" she asked, crossing her arms at Kane.

Kane shrugged, "I thought it would be more fun this way."

Kailani rolled her eyes and told Ash, "Just don't let any of this freak you out, okay?"

He nodded, unsure of if he would be able to make good on that promise. The unknown made him nervous. Kailani held her hands out to the boys and they each took one.

The water splashed around Ash's ankles as Kailani led them back into the ocean. He was becoming more nervous.

Their heads submerged completely just after Ash took a deep breath. He looked at his friends and Kailani giggled at his puffed-up cheeks. "You can breathe," he heard her say, albeit muffled.

He took a breath and was able to breathe normally despite feeling the water on his face. The tension in his nerves seemed to relax a little as he realized he wasn't going to drown.

As the sand of the ocean floor sloped down, their feet lifted, and then a magical force began propelling them through the water. It had to be Kailani; her Atlantean magic was amazing.

Ash had no idea how fast they were moving, but after a couple of minutes, he was able to see the vast expanse of deep blue ocean. The ocean floor disappeared and all that could be seen was water and the occasional sign of marine life. Minute particles floated past as the water sloshed around them.

Their acceleration came to a halt and then they descended into the depths. It would have been pitch dark if not for the bioluminescent life that teemed everywhere.

A palace bigger than anything Ash could have imagined came into view. It reminded him of the old Atlantis. The massive walls and pillars looked to be crafted from sand and reefs, crawling with glowing blue life forms.

Ash's jaw slackened from the awe it struck in him. He looked over at Kailani as their feet touched down on the ocean floor. The girl grinned fiercely. "Welcome to the new Atlantis," she said.

Welcome to New Atlantis

"This is amazing," Ash marveled at the magnificent edifice. "I was wondering where all the Atlanteans had gone off to." Apart from the main palace stretched miles worth of smaller buildings. It was an entire city that made New York seem feeble.

Kailani had let their hands go. A brief flutter of panic hit Ash until he noticed he could still breathe and the crushing pressure that was to be expected at such depths did not assault him.

"The sea calls to us," she told him. "The Guardians offered to expand the homes on Asmaria, but this is where we belong."

"I'm willing to bet King Gabriel will be thrilled to see you're awake," Kane offered.

Stepping through the threshold, Ash could see a grand hall with high ceilings and pillars made of rock and reef. Sconces lined the walls where flames were ablaze, lighting the vast chamber. As his body crossed over into the hall, the ocean water seemed to disappear.

The king sat upon his throne at the far end, deliberating with his council. He waved them away and jumped to his feet when he noticed Ash. He began walking towards them with a vivacious smile.

He spread his arms wide. "Ash, my boy. Welcome back to the land of the waking!"

Ash dropped to a knee, head bowed. "Thank you, King Gabriel."

"You needn't be so formal here. Rise and allow me to show you around the city."

Ash stood back up. "That sounds great!"

"Come. We have much to catch you up on!" Gabriel clapped a meaty hand on Ash's shoulder.

The kingdom of Atlantis stretched far and wide; the city was teeming with foot traffic along the ocean floor. Ash would have never fathomed the vastness of the city despite all the magic he had seen in the past couple of years.

"Where's the Atlanteum?" Ash asked, smiling.

The king sighed, "Alas, it has yet to be constructed. For now, we do most of our training on Asmaria. It's important that we all hone our skills together as a united people. We must be ready when the coming war begins."

"Right," Ash replied. "I guess I hadn't thought of it that way."

"The Atlanteum will be resurrected again one day." Gabriel put his hands on his hips as they stood atop a hill, looking over the city.

Ash turned to Kailani. "How is it we aren't drowning right now?"

"To put it simply, the seas are ours to command. It does that which we require when we require it. Our gods made it so."

Kane shook his head gently. "All the time I've spent hanging around this girl, and I still can't understand her sometimes." That warranted a swift punch to the arm from Kailani.

Ash laughed, turning back to the king. "King Gabriel, what is your plan in all of this?"

"I plan to do whatever the Guardians ask of me. When the time to fight Aros and his army comes, we Atlanteans shall be ready." He took a deep breath, seeming to steel himself for what he was about to say.

"I understand that your father is somewhat of a General for this demon king. How does that sit with you?"

Ash mulled it over. He tried not to dwell on it too often. He'd never known his biological father in the slightest. The brief time he'd spent with Augustus hadn't been of his own volition. The man was a coward in Ash's eyes.

"He's an enemy of Asmaria," Ash said. "I don't know if you've met my adoptive father, Rick, but *he* is my father. Not Augustus. If he stands in my way, I'll show him the mercy he deserves. None."

Awkward silence.

"Alrighty," Kane interceded. "Enough with the melodrama. There's something else Ash needs to see before the day is over."

They all looked to him. Ash asked, "And that is?"

"The situation with the Great Tree."

They bid King Gabriel farewell as they marched back through the massive palace. Once outside, Kailani took their hands again and they rocketed through the water.

Ash's stomach somersaulted as his brain concocted scenarios that would cause the need for him to see the Tree. It had been impossible to tell by Kane's words alone; his expression didn't surrender anything. Although, Ash couldn't think of a time when the word 'situation' was used in a positive manner.

Finally, the beach came back into view. They marched through the sand, sopping wet, and Ash wished there was a water mage nearby.

Lucky for him, his wish was being granted. His stomach did another flip as Quinn approached with that bright smile. Her tan had deepened more than he remembered.

"Hey, guys," she said. "What's going on?"

Kane answered, "We're taking Ash to see the Tree."

Ash found that the 'situation' was indeed not good, thanks to Quinn's smile faltering as she said, "Oh."

What's Up With the Tree?

The way to the Great Tree was all too familiar to Ash. No amount of time asleep could take that away from him. His heart rammed against his ribs, threatening to lunge out of his chest as they grew closer to the Tree. None of them spoke; the only sound that could be heard was the Asmarian wildlife and leaves crunching beneath their feet.

The foliage of the Great Tree was the first thing Ash noticed. The once vibrant colors were beginning to dull. Gethin—the Queen of the Fae—had given her life in the first war against Aros. She cast a spell that would immortalize her in the form of the Great Tree, passing magic along to the Asmarians.

There were two mages looking out for the Great Tree now. The sight of the Tree grew more dismal the closer Ash got. There was a spot on the trunk where the bark was being folded away as if a door lay under all its layers.

Ash reached out to touch the Tree, but Quinn grabbed his hand. She let go just as quickly and Ash thought he saw her blush.

"What's wrong with the Tree?" he asked.

Quinn shrugged. "No one knows. The consensus is that the spell the Atlanteans gave to us is wearing off. She's going to die."

Ash shook his head. "No, no, no. This can't be happening. Did they try to replicate the spell?"

Kailani answered, "Yes. It didn't work. Our Shaman tried tinkering with the formula as well, but so far nothing has slowed the progress of whatever is happening."

Ash reached out again and Quinn said, "Stop, Ash. The Guardians have forbidden anyone from touching the Tree." The mages standing guard leaned in as if they would step in if Ash didn't listen.

Ash looked at Kane, a knowing look passing between them.

"What?" Quinn began. "What was that look?"

The two boys smirked. Kane said, "Since when have we known our lovable friend here to listen to the Guardians?"

Ash turned back to the tree. "Please, don't," Quinn begged.

This was not the time to be a stand-up citizen. They needed answers. Even the two guards looked curious to see what would happen.

He inched his hand forward until his fingers connected with the Great Tree. Nothing. He felt nothing. No visions, no jolts of energy.

"Weird," he noted, pulling his hand away. "Nothing happened. No vision or message. No connection." His head dropped slightly.

"Well," Kane began, "at least nothing bad happened this time."

"That's true," Quinn agreed. "Are you guys hungry? My mom should be making dinner right about now."

Ash smiled despite feeling dejected. He wanted to help the Great Tree, but was at a loss for the time being. "I can eat."

Raimir? Ash reached out with his mind. *Are you there?*

He waited a moment and then, *I am here.* The deep voice of his feathery friend rumbled in his brain.

When can I see you?

Raimir avoided the question. *What of the Guardians? What punishment did they hand you?*

Ash chuckled, *Community service. I haven't done anything too crazy so far.*

Are you practicing with your abilities?

A bit, he admitted.

It is imperative that you become stronger with your magical prowess, Raimir began to lecture. *We have a plan for you to surpass your limits, but you must ensure that your body is ready.*

Ash rolled his eyes. *Can you stop beating around the bush already? Just tell me what this huge training secret is. I can handle it, I swear.*

I know you can handle it. He paused for so long that Ash was about to interject, but before he could, Raimir broke the silence. *Do you remember what I told you about where I'm from?*

A little, Ash said.

It is an ethereal realm beyond the human mind's comprehension. Most of the beings on your planet believe that there is only one dimension, but this is incorrect. There are multiple, so many that you would not be able to number them. I reside in one of these other dimensions.

Right, Ash said, wondering where the story was going. *What's the point of telling me all that?*

Raimir huffed. *The point is that I shall bring you here to get stronger. Strong enough to defeat the demon.*

A nervous jolt went through him. He asked, *Bring me to your world? Why?*

Yes. There are energies in this plane that you cannot fathom. You will become more powerful than any other mage in your world. In doing so, you will be able to bring down the demon king.

And you're sure of that? Ash was sure of only one thing: he had failed time after time to stop Aros.

I am positive.

Okay. I trust you. Ash trusted the giant falcon more than he did most humans. *When will this happen?*

That day has yet to be decided and I will need to see that you can handle the trip here. Hone your skills daily, and soon we will be reunited.

"Ash, are you listening?" Rick asked.

Ash couldn't focus on much of anything; he was constantly replaying Raimir's words in his head. Fear plagued him. The fear of not being strong enough to enter the beast's realm. The fear that he may become more powerful and still lose to Aros and his father.

"Sorry," Ash apologized. "What'd you say?"

Rick's eyebrows knit with worry. "I asked how the community service was going."

"Oh. It's not bad." He poked at his food with one hand. The other was beneath the table twirling purple lightning between the fingers.

"I can tell that something is on your mind," Rick said. "Feel like sharing?"

Ash considered it. He decided that if he couldn't tell Rick, then he shouldn't even be contemplating going.

"I spoke with Raimir last night," he told him. Then tapped the side of his head when Rick looked confused.

"Oh, right," Rick said. "Go on."

Ash shared everything he and Raimir had discussed. When he was done, he stared at his plate.

"Do you think you'll go?" Rick asked.

"I was kind of hoping you'd make the decision for me," Ash admitted with a laugh.

Rick smiled. "Not a chance, bud. As we both know, you're much stronger than I am these days. Your magical abilities are amazing. I can tell you what I *think* you should do."

Ash nodded. Rick continued, "I think you should take every chance possible to destroy that monster forever. I won't force you to go or to stay, but I'll have your back with whatever decision you make."

A wave of relief rolled over him. It was great to have someone in his corner no matter what. "Thanks, Rick. I think I'll go. Raimir says he's positive that he can make me strong enough to beat Aros. I just have to convince the Guardians to allow it."

Rick shrugged, saying, "If they try to stop you, I say you go anyway. They aren't gods. They don't always know what the best choice for you is. Only you can make the best choice for yourself."

That settled it. Ash would begin regaining his magical endurance. He would get back into the routine of pushing himself as hard as he could go, and when he's fully prepared, he will call back out to Raimir.

Inception

Kane continued to grow his abilities with controlling wind magic. It would seem that training all the other wind mages in Asmaria every day had its perks. Not even Bora could compete with his magical aptitude. Her leadership abilities still greatly outshone his, but Kane knew he would be a Guardian one day. Just as he'd always dreamed.

Some would probably attribute his skill to the Atlantean rings he wore on his thumbs, but he knew differently. Most of the time he would take the rings off so that his true, raw, magical ability would be honed.

With him becoming a leader amongst his peers Kane pushed himself harder than ever. His strength had increased so substantially that he could conjure winds powerful enough to rip fully grown trees from the ground. He knew he was capable because he'd done it.

The physical exertion that he'd inflicted upon himself had caused him to pass out. When he awoke, he found himself with a bloody nose beside the felled tree.

Kane left the tree and the jungle and returned to his home. That same night was the first time he had a visitor in his dreams. Well, a visitor that wasn't a pretty girl.

It had started as any normal dream; he was wearing the garb of the Guardian of wind. His fellow mages stood before him, recognizing his leadership. It was strange, but he felt that he was more powerful than any other on the island. Then the dream shifted.

The bright hues of daylight vanished and the world turned dark, cold. He gripped his arms as he shivered. Shackles dangled from his wrists as well as from the wrists of those around him. They stood in a field of what looked like burned wheat. The ground was blackened and smoke filled his nostrils, although the earth beneath his bare feet was just barely warm.

A dais was erected with a throne made of bones and flesh, and sitting atop it was none other than Aros.

The demon king looked down at them with his purely white eyes, an evil, gleeful grin spread across his face. He threw his head back as he laughed.

The dream shifted again. This time Kane was surrounded by his family and friends in his family's home. He tried to speak, but none could hear him. They feasted at the long table in their dining room. Aros sat at the head of the table, eyes boring into Kane's soul.

"What do you want from me?" Kane shouted at the demon king. His voice sounded weird to him, distorted.

Aros smiled and said, "It's simple. I want you."

That first dream ended just as abruptly as it had begun. He sat up in his bed, sweating profusely. He took a walk to calm his mind that night.

That was six months into Ash's coma, and since then, he'd had a similar dream every night. The sweating and angst stopped after a while and he found that he would fall back asleep if he tried. The dreams never returned for a second showing within the same night.

So far Kane had gathered that Aros was offering him a deal. He wanted the mage to join him, and in return he would give Kane everything he desired. Kane would become the most powerful mage to live. He would lead an army of his own and his friends and family would be spared from the torment that the rest of the world would endure.

However, if Kane refused, the suffering he will endure will be worse than any other human on Earth.

A plan was forming in Kane's mind but he wasn't sure anyone else would go along with it. No one, except maybe one person.

Ash.

He had a knack for getting into trouble and breaking rules.

Kane promised himself that he wouldn't go through with the plan if he couldn't get at least one person to back him up. He didn't want to be labeled a traitor for no reason.

The plot forming in his mind was perhaps the most danger-ous plan he'd ever come up with. It wasn't fully formed yet, though. Kane would wait until he was sure he could convince Ash to support him.

Ash drank some water infused with heala. Sweat rolled down the sides of his face and slicked his back. He was taking a break from hurling bolts of lightning at the metal targets on the training field.

"Hey," Quinn said.

He jumped, startled as she snuck up behind him.

"Geez, you scared me."

"I'm not that scary looking," she jested.

"You're not scary looking at all," Ash said. He felt his cheeks get warm, although not as warm as they would have been prior to his coma. He smiled at her and she returned it.

She tucked a loose strand of hair behind her ear as she asked, "How are you settling back into the semi-normal life of the only lightning mage in Asmaria?"

He held his hand open, allowing the purple arcs to travel around his fingers. "It's been tough, honestly. I feel as weak as I used to when I first learned I could do this, except I still have all the knowledge I've gained. My body just can't seem to keep up with all the energy it takes."

"I'm sorry. I'm sure with a little time everything will go back to normal."

Ash looked at his toes. "I'm not sure I have that much time."

"What do you mean?"

He looked around, checking to make sure no one was close enough to overhear him. "Can you keep a secret?"

"Of course," she said, smiling.

"I've spoken with Raimir," he began. "He plans to bring me to his realm to make me stronger, but I need to make my body and mind as strong as possible here before I'm ready to go there. And… I'm scared."

Her brows had pinched together. "Well, I can see why. We have no idea what could be waiting for you in this other world. We don't know if you can even survive over there."

"That's not entirely why I'm scared."

"Then why?" she asked.

"I've done nothing but fail." His shoulders slumped. "From the moment I learned of this ability, I've failed every step of the way. What if I can't become strong enough? What if I fail to beat Aros, *again*?"

She grabbed Ash's hand, looking into his eyes. "I have every faith that you will be strong enough when the time comes to face him again. Remember, you're not alone, Ash. All of us have your back."

He nodded, a sense of relief coming over him. "Thanks. I just hope the Guardians don't put up too much of a fight when I bring up going with Raimir."

She shrugged. "Surely by now, they know that you're stubborn enough to ignore them and go anyway."

He laughed, "That's true." They looked at each other for a moment, and then Ash began again, "Hey, I wanted to talk to you about something else."

"I'm all ears."

"Do you—"

Before Ash could finish, a beacon of gold light blasted into the atmosphere from the center of the island. The two of them jumped to their feet, staring at the nearly blinding light. After a couple of seconds, a shockwave of energy smacked into them. They stumbled but didn't fall.

"What is that?" he asked, panic in his voice as they stared at the pillar of gold.

"It's the Great Tree," she replied.

The Beacon

ugustus munched on the rancid scraps that had been tossed down into the pit that he called home. His fingers were as good as they were probably going to be without proper medical attention. When he was done he made another tally on the stone wall next to him with a jagged rock.

Over a year had gone by since Aros tossed him into the dark, dull prison. A pulsing ache throbbed in his hands as he closed his eyes, leaning back against the wall. The pit was roughly ten feet in diameter and, by his estimation, thirty feet deep.

Shivers haunted his body. Finally, he was ready to try to remedy at least that ailment.

Augustus took a couple of deep breaths, feeling the power tingle within him. He pulled and it roared to life. Flames no bigger than that of a candle ignited on all of his fingertips.

He smiled. His smile grew until it became laughter which transcended into tears. It was time to attempt to break free.

Augustus didn't know where the dark master had gone, and he didn't care all that much. The Asmarians would take him back, if not only for the information he harbored.

The fire mage stood and stepped to the center of the pit. It would take a lot of force and magical effort to create a blast of fire that would lift him out of the hole.

Palms facing the ground, he summoned everything within him; flames erupted from his hands and he felt his feet begin to rise.

"Ah!" he screamed as he fell back the few inches he'd gained.

Augustus' hands curled towards his body as he grimaced. Pain wrecked him. It was as if his hands had been broken all over again. However, he knew they weren't really.

Laughter echoed down from above. He spared a glance upward. The face of the demon king glared down at him in the dim light.

"Going somewhere, Augustus?" he asked.

He dared not answer. Any answer would have resulted in a harsher punishment.

"Very well," Aros said. He chuckled, "You will never escape. You shall watch your boy burn, and then you will join him."

Then he sealed off the hole at the top with shadows. Pitch darkness was all that Augustus could see. He wanted to create a flame but his hands were still throbbing and he was afraid to try again so soon.

Augustus slunk to the dirty ground, wrapping his arms around his knees as he pulled them to his chest. It's such a funny thing that he dislikes the darkness so much, even after all the time he'd spent there.

It was impossible to tell how many days had gone by. The veil of shadow never left the pit Augustus was trapped in and the scraps he was accustomed to had stopped coming after the night he tried to escape.

Aros did not visit, nor did anyone else. Not that there was

anyone else left.

The demon king absorbed every last soul from the members of the Forbidden. Augustus reminisced on the few friendships he'd made from within the organization.

Many of them weren't bad people, but were lost. The group existed only because of the bitterness Asmarians often felt at not being granted magic. Now, because of Augustus, they were all dead. It was all his fault. All of it.

He was the one who brought Aros back. He was the man who'd allowed the dark lord to ride his body for so long. He was the *coward* who couldn't say no to the demon king.

Augustus rested his chin against his chest as tears slid down his cheeks.

He began talking to his late wife, unsure of if she could hear him, and too worn to care if it made him crazy. "Look at me now, Iris." Flames licked his palms, illuminating the area around him. "Better yet, don't. You would hate me. Although, I wouldn't blame you."

He cast the orb of fire to slowly drift around the pit. "You always said that I was a great man. If only you knew what I was fated to do."

Augustus pulled his knees in tightly and wrapped his arms around them. "I wish you had been able to stop me. I wish you would have been strong enough to end me, right then and there. Of course, Aros was already residing in me then."

His mind flashed back to the night. He tricked Iris into leaving Asmaria with him and their baby boy. Allowing Aros to use his body to kill Iris was one of the hardest things he'd ever done. Leaving Ash on that park bench was worse.

After we kill the girl, you must leave the boy. This is the only way I can save them, he remembered Aros telling him.

Augustus stood and faced the wall. *How could I have been so stupid?* he cursed himself. He pulled his head back and then slammed it against the rocks. His head swirled from the impact.

He rubbed the knot that was forming and promptly drifted off as the floating ball of fire winked out. Darkness encapsulated the fire mage yet again.

The Stronger Mage

A week had gone by and she still hadn't woken from her slumber. Her chest rose and fell in a slow rhythm. Ash and Quinn weren't the first to arrive at the Great Tree—which no longer stood. A black circle of singed dirt replaced its massive trunk and only the faintest of signs of its foliage were scattered around.

A small crowd was already there, bearing witness to the tragedy or miracle that had occurred, however, it was too soon to tell which one it would be. The gold light destroyed the Tree entirely, and yet, every mage's magic remained. The island did not fall into the sea, nor did its ground split open.

When the light faded, all that remained was a single girl wearing an emerald, green dress. Her luscious brown hair was fanned out on the ground beneath her and her arms lay at her side as if she were in a coffin.

Ash had heard murmurs scattering through the scant crowd.

"What happened to the Tree?"

"Who is that?"

To which he answered, "That's Gethin."

The Guardians arrived shortly after, checking for a pulse and that she was breathing. They answered none of the questions that were hurled at them. Ash figured it was because they didn't know anything more than anyone else.

They spirited the limp body of their goddess away, leaving nothing but confusion in their wake.

Even the Atlanteans knew something was awry; the king and his entourage showed up just as the Guardians left with Gethin. Gabriel had gone pale when they told him what had happened.

"Do you have any idea what this means?" Ash had asked him. A solemn shake of his head was the only reply he received.

Since then, Gethin lay in the hospital with the healers monitoring her constantly, waiting and hoping that she would wake soon.

The Guardians were holding a meeting with all of Asmaria in the Capitol building. The atmosphere was unusual in the fact that their mage leaders did not have to quiet the crowd. The excitement, fear, or whatever it was kept the chatter down to a minimum.

Bora stepped forward, looking around at the faces. Ash had a nervous feeling in the pit of his stomach. She began, "Fellow Asmarians. I probably don't have to tell you what this meeting is all about, but for any who may be in the dark, the Great Tree is no more."

She paused, allowing everyone to take in her words. "The one whom we all have inherited our abilities from has emerged from the Great Tree in what is reminiscent of her old form. King Gabriel of Atlantis can share a little more on that." Ash hadn't even noticed him standing off to the side.

Bora turned to him and held out a hand. An inviting gesture. "King Gabriel, if you would, please."

He nodded as he stepped forward. His voice boomed

around the cavernous theater, "Many of you I have not had the pleasure of meeting, however, I am *far* older than I appear. I was there the first time the Asmarians faced Aros. I knew Gethin well. The spell she cast with her last breath obliterated Aros—obviously not for good—and turned herself into the Great Tree, immortalizing herself.

"This version of Gethin that has emerged is slightly different; she's taller, for one thing." He smiled, probably remembering old times with his friend. "Also, when I visited her, the power I could feel was immense. Greater than anything I've ever felt. It is my belief that this Tree was a chrysalis of sorts and that Gethin has morphed into a more powerful version of herself."

That did it. Murmurs rippled through the crowd. Quinn turned to Ash, saying, "Can you believe that?" Her smile and eyes were bright and wide. Ash couldn't help but smile back.

"I don't know what to believe," he said.

"Silence!" Gabriel's voice called out.

When it was silent again, Leena stepped forward. "We understand that this information isn't solid. All we have are theories and those are confusing for us as well. If and when Gethin awakes, we shall let all of you know. Dismissed."

"Should we go see her?" Quinn asked.

"I was thinking the same thing," Ash admitted.

He wanted to touch her hand or something. Touching the Tree had given him visions in the past and allowed him to speak with Gethin. Maybe this would do the same thing.

When the two of them approached her room in the hospital, they noticed there were a couple of mages standing guard outside. They tried to enter as if it was normal, but the mages wouldn't let them in.

"Sorry, kids," one of them said. "Guardian's orders. No one

gets in that room without approval."

Ash looked at him funny. "But we have approval. They didn't tell you?"

The other one smirked. "Nice try. We're not falling for that."

Quinn crossed her arms and huffed. Ash shrugged and said, "It was worth a try. Come on, let's go."

After leaving the hospital, Quinn left to go help her parents with some errands. Ash found Kane walking down the street with Kailani.

"Mind if I borrow him for a minute?" Ash asked her.

She smiled, saying, "As long as you bring him back."

"I should probably get my wind mages together instead of spending all my time under the sea anyway. Talk to you tomorrow?" Kailani nodded and walked away looking somewhat disappointed.

"So, what's up?" Kane asked.

"I've already spoken with Quinn about this," he began, "but I wanted your input too." He took a deep breath. "I spoke with Raimir a while back. He says that he can help to make me stronger. Strong enough to defeat Aros for good."

Kane smiled, patting Ash on the back. "That's awesome!"

Ash nodded. "Yeah, it is. Except he needs to take me to his realm which sounds cool, other than the fact that I have to get strong enough to survive the trip and survive in that dimension."

"Well, that's not so awesome," Kane admitted. Worry knitting his brows.

"Right. What if I can't become strong enough to survive and it's all for nothing?"

Kane sighed, looking out across the training field as they

approached it. "Ash, I know I joke around and pester you a lot, but you're already one of the strongest people I know. Remember the prophecy?"

He did and he hated it. He nodded.

"I wholeheartedly believe that you are meant to save this world," Kane said. "That means that the power to save us is already inside of you. You just need to access it."

Ash smiled, feeling warm and fuzzy from the sudden compliments.

"Of course, you'll always be second to me," Kane told him with a smirk. Fuzzy feeling gone. Joy took its place.

"I needed that," Ash said. "I told myself I wasn't going to agree to go unless you, Quinn, and Rick gave your approval. So that's settled. I'm going."

"What about the Guardians?" Kane asked.

Ash grinned, "What about them?"

After laughing, Kane said, "I knew you weren't going to care about their opinions."

Ash punched him in the arm. "It makes me sound bad when you say it like that." In truth, Ash cared more than anyone knew what the Guardians thought of him. He just hadn't been great at showing it.

The two laughed and walked around the training field in silence for a minute before Kane said, "I have something similar to run by you as well."

"Go for it," Ash replied. How could he *possibly* have something similar on his mind?

Kane stopped in front of Ash and placed his hands on his shoulders. The concern on his face worried Ash. "Whether you agree to this or not, you can't tell anyone. Okay?"

"Okay. What's going on?"

Kane pulled back and took a deep breath before revealing what he had planned. "I want to infiltrate Aros' army."

"I'm sorry," Ash said, shaking his head. "You *what?*"

"I know," Kane replied as he began pacing in circles. "It sounds crazy. I know that. Just think about it for a second. In case you haven't noticed, we don't have a sure-fire way of killing him for good. A man on the inside would be invaluable."

"And what happens when he makes you prove your loyalty? Or figures out that you're a spy?" Ash argued.

"Fair point," Kane nodded. "He's not going to figure me out, I'm too good. And I would do whatever it takes to bring him down permanently."

"Even if it means killing an innocent person?"

Kane didn't answer. He didn't need to. The look on his face was enough for Ash to see the truth. Was he serious?

"This isn't like you, Kane," he said. "Where is this coming from?"

Kane slipped his Atlantean rings over his fingers and the symbols began glowing faintly. *What is he thinking?*

A slight breeze began blowing in. Kane's bangs whipped around his face. "You think you know me, Ash, but you only know what I've allowed you to see. You've never seen me for who I truly am."

Ash didn't know what to do. He pleaded, "Kane, you're my best friend. Don't do this! I don't want to hurt you." Ash pulled at the magic in his gut, allowing it to run through him. His hair began to rise from the static.

The face that peered into him was not that of his friend, nor of someone he even recognized. What was happening? It all came from nowhere. One second Kane is normal, and the next he's a deranged lunatic.

Kane smirked, confidence apparent on his face. "You were out of commission for a while. You don't even understand how strong I am now." His hands began to whirl around as his wind magic activated.

Brothers Fight

Kane whipped a powerful gust at Ash; flipping through the air, he landed hard on his back. Kane controlled the winds, lifting Ash from the ground and hovering a few feet in the air.

Ash gasped out, "Why are you doing this?"

Kane answered, "This is the only way! If I join Aros, I'll be able to save everyone!"

"Whatever he's told you, it's a lie! You have to know that!" Ash argued.

With a grunt, Kane thrust his hands out. Ash flew another several yards away but was able to land on his feet before doing a somersault.

Kane knew he would win this battle, especially with Ash not being as strong as he used to be. However, he had to make it look real. With each blow Kane dealt, the bonds of their friendship loosened. He had to hope that Ash would forgive him when it was all over.

Suddenly, Ash's arm reached out to nothing and the magical Atlantean bow, Beithir, snapped into his hand. Kane reached behind his back and freed a karambit from its sheath as he began to charge Ash.

Kane could feel the crackle in the air as Ash nocked the bow with an arrow made of amethyst lightning. He loosed it; the bolt rocketed towards Kane. The rubber in the handle of the karambit kept Kane from taking any damage as he slashed at the bolt. It was just slow enough for him to see.

The bow vanished, the small white tattoo reappeared on Ash's arm as he summoned his magical power. Lightning erupted from his fingertips as he thrust them forward, striking the ground under Kane's feet.

Kane had launched himself with a blast of wind just at the right time to avoid being struck. He threw the karambit at Ash. That type of weapon wasn't great for throwing, but it didn't matter when the thrower could manipulate the air around the blade.

It looked like it was going to miss Ash and the boy made the mistake of ignoring it as it sailed past him. With a flick of his wrist, Kane summoned a small wind to redirect the karambit. The blade changed direction and planted itself in Ash's back.

Ash would be fine. Kane was a professional, after all, and knew how to not injure people too badly.

Kane landed back on the ground in front Ash. His heart hurt for his friend as he arched, trying feebly to get away from the pain he felt in his back. *I'm sorry.*

He punched Ash in the stomach and ripped his blade free as the boy doubled over. Kane slid the karambit back into its sheath. He sighed. "You should have just agreed, Ash. This all could have been much easier on the both of us."

Ash fell to his knees and Kane nearly crumbled when his friend lifted his head with tears balancing on his lower eyelids, doing their best to not fall. "How could you do this to us? To me?" he asked.

Kane just shook his head and turned around, walking away briskly. He couldn't let him see how bad that had hurt. He needed everyone to believe the lie.

Snap.

The sound of Beithir being called to Ash's hand.

Kane spun around as a purple arrow was released. He was too close and too slow. The bolt may have pierced his heart if he hadn't flinched away. It hit him near the shoulder, just below the collar bone.

The pain was instant and immense. It seared his flesh like a hot knife being driven into him. He screamed out from the agony and it came out like a rageful roar. Ash nocked another lightning arrow.

The pain twisted and turned into anger, rippling through Kane's body. The pain he could see in Ash's eyes only fed the rage. People began entering the training field. He could see them in his peripherals. They would think it was nothing more than a friendly bout.

Kane wouldn't get another opportunity to let so many people see him become a traitor.

Ash released the arrow. Kane dodged and slashed his hand through the air. A wind so sharp that it could cut into glass produced a laceration across Ash's chest. With another scream, Kane pulled at his magic with nearly everything he had.

The gale-force winds that he conjured began flinging the other mages and tearing the equipment buildings from their foundations that were placed around the training field.

Kane could feel the ground beneath him begin to rumble. *Time to go.*

As quickly as the damaging winds had arrived, they were gone. Before anyone could apprehend him, Kane blasted himself away. He saw some of the other wind mages pursuing him, but they would never catch up. He ignored the pain in his shoulder.

All that was left for Kane now was to seek out Aros and infiltrate his ranks. He would convince the demon king that he was joining his side and do whatever was asked of him. In the end, he would have the answer for ending the beast's life for good.

Ash's chest was on fire. The pain he felt was leagues above the pain in his back. He never knew being sliced open by wind could be so horrible. He laid on his back whimpering as another mage tended to the wound.

"Don't worry, kid," he said. "You'll be alright."

The extensive agony in his body did not compare to that of his heart.

How could he do this?

Kane just threw away their friendship as easily as if he'd been throwing away a piece of garbage.

More mages crowded around him and began carrying him to the hospital.

"So, he told you he was going to join Aros?" Avani asked Ash as he lay in the bed. His chest and back were fully wrapped and he had been ordered to eat some heala and drink water until his wounds closed.

"At first," Ash began, "It seemed like he was doing it just so that we'd have a man on the inside. Of course, I told him how crazy that was and then his whole demeanor changed."

"Changed how?" Dihren asked.

Ash sighed. "I've never seen him so angry. It was like he

wanted to kill me for standing in his way. I have to admit, I was scared. He had this wild look in his eyes as if he'd gone mad or something. It was like he *wanted* to join Aros for real. I don't really know how else to explain it."

Ash looked between the Guardians as their silence began to weigh on him. He couldn't be certain of what they were thinking, but they all looked worried.

"There's something else I need to admit to you all," Ash said, causing the leaders to look up from their thoughts.

"Go on," Bora ordered.

Ash wrung his hands together. This conversation would determine if he was going to ignore the Guardian's commands yet again.

He told them of the things Raimir shared with him. He spared no detail and, when he had finished, Avani told him, "Allow us some time to discuss this matter. We will give you an answer after you've healed. Until then, get some rest, and try not to think about Kane too much."

"The betrayal of a friend can be a most difficult thing to bear," Dihren said. "However, you still have others you can lean on. You're not alone in any of this." The fire mage put a hand on Ash's shoulder and squeezed affectionately. Ash hadn't spent much time around the new Guardian since his return to the waking world, but decided then that he liked the man.

"Thank you," he said. "All of you."

They each offered Ash a nod and disappeared from his room. He could hear their hushed tones as they gathered in Gethin's room which was only a couple of doors down from him.

Ash found an immense weight had lifted from his chest, and relief washed over him. He hadn't expected the Guardians to respond so lightly about him leaving to train with Raimir.

Later, Rick was visiting him, and Ash told his adoptive father all that had happened that day. Rick put a hand to Ash's forehead and said, "I'm just glad you're okay."

"I have to bring him back," Ash said. He hadn't mentioned this to the Guardians, but Ash had every intention of going after his friend.

"I don't think that's a good idea," Rick admitted.

"Why not?"

Rick sighed, rubbing the back of his neck. "Not to bring the mood down any more than it already is, but Kane has a huge head start on you. If he makes it to Aros before you can catch up, I don't see how you'd avoid a fight with him. We both know what happened the last time you fought Aros. All I'm saying is, take some time, rest, and when you're strong enough, let Raimir turn you into a beast." He smiled at that.

Rick went on, "Then, take the fight to Aros and send him back to Hell."

"I think I can agree to that," Ash said with a grin.

"Good," Rick stood from the chair he was sitting in. "I've got some work to do, so get some sleep, and I'll see you tomorrow."

"I'll try."

Rick left and Ash peered through the window of his room. He looked away and closed his eyes. He wasn't sure if sleep was going to evade him or not; he was exhausted, but his mind was working overtime.

He knew he had dozed off, but a clamoring in the hall startled him awake. Dim moonlight shown through his window. He waited, but nothing else happened aside from the faint chatter he could hear. Assuming it was the hospital staff, he closed his eyes again.

Then, a soft, warm glow tickled his eyelids. A deep red ignited his closed eyes as if the sun were shining down on him. He cracked his eyes open to find Gethin standing in his doorway. Her brown hair and verdant dress rippled as if the wind was blowing through them. Her vibrant, colorful eyes were wide, looking panicked, and her skin had a golden glow about it that was beginning to recede.

Ash slowly sat up, grimacing from the pain of moving, as Gethin crept towards him. His heart was racing, he didn't know what to do. His mouth opened as if to speak, but words eluded him.

Her hand lifted towards him, a ball of light forming in her palm. It elongated, shifting into a vibrant sword crafted from different shades of yellow, white, and gold light.

Gethin's fingers curled around the hilt of the light sword as it continued to expand. The tip stopped just short of Ash's throat.

Her voice sounded different from what Ash remembered. In the visions, she had sounded as if multiple people were speaking in unison. This time it was just a singular voice, however, she sounded ethereal nonetheless. "Tell me where I am and why I shouldn't slay you here and now."

On The Run

Kane hadn't left Asmaria but a few times throughout his 18 years of life, and now he didn't care. There were times where he wondered what living elsewhere would be like, and wished he could visit the cities of non-magical folk. Having done that now, he didn't much care for it.

His plan hadn't originally been to have a big showdown with Ash, it just kind of led to that. There was no time to grab gear or anything besides the clothes on his back. After learning how much he stuck out among the crowd of people, he quickly found a discount store and ditched his mage clothes.

Thievery wasn't something he was proud of, but he didn't know what else to do. He didn't even know where he was. It's not as if the normies could stop him. Sure, they have more advanced weapons, but magic would always outclass anything they could come up with, or so he hoped.

Some food, and medicine for his arm, were the last items he swiped before setting out to search for Aros. Kane wasn't sure where he was, but was glad to hear that the people around him spoke the same language.

Can't believe I let him hit me, Kane chastised himself as

he examined his wound. There was a small hole that went straight through his shoulder. It wasn't bleeding, luckily, but was scorched around the edges. Now that his adrenaline had worn off, the pain came with a vengeance.

He sat on a park bench putting bandages over the wounds, when suddenly, someone snatched the plastic bag that held his food items.

The thief sprinted away as Kane stood from the bench. "Really?" Kane called out to the back of the man and began his pursuit.

The guy was fast but he was a normie. Kane waited until there weren't too many watchful eyes before using his magic. A shock of pain jolted through his shoulder and left arm as he blasted himself into the air with a gust of wind. He landed gently in front of the thief, roughly ten feet or so.

The man skidded to a halt. "What? H-how?" he stammered.

Kane held out his hand. "I'm magic, man. Now give me what's mine and I'll let you walk away unscathed."

The confusion of the man seemed to leave him as he scowled and pulled out a large knife from his waistband. "Walk away, pretty boy, or I'll gut you like a fish."

Kane knew then why Asmaria kept to itself. He put his hands in his pockets and slowly approached. When he was within reach, the man swung at him with the knife. Kane ducked under his arm, spinning around behind him, and kicked the bend of his knee.

The man stumbled forward but didn't fall. He whirled around, knife poised to strike again. "Ahh!" he cried as he lunged for the white-haired boy.

Kane's right hand flew up to face the knife. He summoned a wind just strong enough to hold it—and the man—in place.

The thief strained, grunting against the force that was pushing against him. His eyes grew wider and sweat slid down his face.

At what point does he realize he's no match for me? Kane wondered.

A smile spread across his face. He thrust his hand forward, sending the man tumbling across the ground. The knife clattered and the food items spilled from the bag.

Kane stood over the man, peering down at him. "You spilled my things."

The man crawled to his knees. "I'm sorry," he clasped his hands together. "Please, let me get it for you. I don't want any trouble."

Kane chuckled, "You tried to kill me—twice I think—and *now* you don't want any trouble? Tell you what, if you can get around the corner of that building by the count of three," he pointed to a building at the end of the street, "then I won't do anything else to you."

The man didn't argue or plead further. He scrambled to his feet and began running away. Kane yelled, "Three!" and sent a blast of wind that tripped the man, causing him to smack his head on the wall, knocking him unconscious.

"Oh well," Kane said, shrugging. He began gathering his things.

"Now, how do I find Aros," he said to himself.

The night was dark and cold as Kane wandered the streets of wherever he was. It was good that he'd read a lot about the normal humans' culture before, otherwise he may have been even more shocked by all the sights he was taking in.

Vehicles astounded him. He thought what a great method

of travel it was. Using wind magic to carry himself had been quite exhausting before the Atlantean rings he now wore.

He found a café of some kind that was still open despite the late hour, so he went inside, shivering as he sat at a table in the corner. A girl who couldn't have been much older than him walked over carrying a pad and pencil.

"What can I get you, dear?" she asked.

Kane wasn't sure what to say. "Uh, I'm not sure," he admitted.

She giggled, "Alright, how about a cup of coffee?"

Kane couldn't recall ever having coffee, but it couldn't have been bad if that was the first thing she offered. He wore a warm smile. "Sure."

"Be right back," she said, spinning around and heading behind a counter.

Kane looked around, taking the room in. There were a couple of other people in the café, speaking quietly to each other. There was a television high up on the wall above him. It was far enough away that he could hear words but couldn't understand what they were saying.

The girl came back and he noted that she bore a tag that read, 'Tracy'.

She sat a cup of black liquid down, saying, "There you go. Cream or sugar?"

Man, I should have done more research before coming here. "Sure," he said, offering that warm smile again. Tracy dipped away as Kane brought the steaming broth to his lips.

The warmth hit him instantly, and it would have been sensational, if not for the bitter taste that assaulted him directly afterward. The face he made couldn't have looked good and he was thankful that Tracy had her back turned. He didn't want to offend anyone.

"Here you go," she said, placing what he assumed was cream and sugar on the table. "Can I get you anything else?"

"Actually," he replied, "I wondered if you might turn that up a bit?" he pointed to the television.

"Certainly. Forgive me if this seems rude, but, that is quite the accent you've got. Where you from?"

He smiled, "Oh, I doubt you've heard of it. It's way out in the Pacific. Not many tourists there."

"Okay, well, welcome to the States," she smiled as she strolled off, gathering a black device and pointing it at the television. The sound increased, finally reaching his ears clearly.

"…here you can see what appears to be a dome of black clouds. Experts haven't been able to identify what it could be, but the theory is that it's some sort of freak storm. Authorities are tentative to get within a kilometer of the phenomena; something about the storm interferes with all electronic frequency."

A couple of miles behind the woman on the screen was a swirling ball of shadow. It was no storm. "There he is," Kane whispered.

After watching for a bit longer, Kane learned that this supernatural manifestation was located in the country of Russia. He didn't know anything about the place.

Kane was becoming increasingly frustrated with not knowing anything about this foreign world.

After adding the cream and sugar to his coffee, it wasn't half bad. He spoke with Tracy about where he could stay for the night. He was able to talk the girl into giving him some money for a room in the cheapest motel she knew of.

The motel wasn't nearly as fancy as the home he was accustomed to, but it would do for the night. The following day he planned to find Aros and swear his false allegiance to him. He was nervous; it was a dangerous game he would be playing, but in the end, he was confident that he was doing the right thing.

Kane laid down, closing his eyes. The long day wore on him. He wanted to drift off as quickly as possible, however, his own thoughts plagued him.

He thought about Ash. A pang of guilt gripped his heart.

Please let this work, please, so that I can return to my friends again, he pleaded. He didn't know to whom.

Soon enough he was fast asleep.

One of those dreams, or rather nightmares, entered his mind.

He wanted to speak directly to the demon king. "Enough!" he shouted, his voice sounding far away from himself, garbled. "Show yourself, Aros! I'm ready to join you!"

Sly laughter tickled his ears. A white tree stood on a hill and it's shadow shifted into the body of Aros. His white eyes bore into Kane. "Come to your senses have you? Realized that there can be only one winner in this war?"

His fists clenched and he seethed, "Yes, I have."

Aros spread his arms wide. "That is splendid to hear, my dear." His smile made Kane's blood boil.

He wasn't sure now if he was going to be strong enough to go through with it. He needed to reign in his nerves or it wouldn't work. "How can I find you?"

Aros clapped his hands. "Do not worry yourself with that, dear boy. I will send for you. Remain at the motel until your ride arrives."

"Ride?" he asked, "What ride?"

With a maniacal laugh, Aros turned into a whisp of black smoke and vanished from sight.

Great, just what I needed, he thought as the dream slowly regressed. *Relying on the demon to pick me up.*

Kane had no more dreams that night, but still, he did not sleep peacefully.

The Queen Rises

Ash held his hands up in surrender, gulping at the knot in his throat so that it was audible. The tip of the light sword was a mere two or three inches away from him. He took a calming breath in through his nose.

"You're in the hospital," he began. "In Asmaria. I'm Ash. Don't you remember me? You know, the boy born of a lightning bolt or whatever?" He chuckled nervously.

She lowered her sword but still held onto it, squinting at him. "Asmaria, you say?" she asked. The sword flicked back up. "And what is a 'hospital'?"

Ash chuckled nervously again. "It's a place for hurt or sick people. Do you really not remember anything?"

The tip of her sword inched dangerously close to him; the heat from the golden blade warmed the skin of his throat. "I will be the one asking the questions here, boy." She lowered the weapon again, taking a step back. "Tell me the truth, I shall know if you lie." She seemed to be waiting for a response, so Ash nodded as he lowered his hands down to his lap.

"My memory is indeed… failing me," she told him. "How long have I been in this hospital? I do not remember it being here before I…" she trailed off.

"I could probably fill you in," Ash said, "but I think we'd better call for the Guardians first."

"What are these Guardians you speak of?"

"They're the four most powerful mages from each magical element on the island." His tone wasn't rude, but rather that the information should be obvious.

She nodded as if remembering something. "Yes. That term seems vaguely familiar; however, I was drawn to you upon my awakening so you will tell me all that I wish to know."

"Okay," he agreed. "Where do you want me to start?"

She seemed to think for a moment, then said, "What do you know of me?"

He chuckled, running his fingers through his hair. "I know that your name is Gethin and that you were once Queen of the Fae."

She grinned. "Merely an alias. I've gone by many names and titles; however, if that is what your people know me as, Gethin will do just fine. Go on."

He nodded. "Keep in mind that I didn't grow up in Asmaria, so my knowledge of its history might be a bit off. From what I remember, Aros was attacking the island and you stopped him. The last spell you cast nearly killed him, but also turned you into a tree."

"What do you mean, 'nearly' killed him?" she asked, with a dubious tone.

"I hate to be the one who breaks it to you," he replied, "but Aros is back and stronger than ever."

Gethin's face went slack and looked pale in the moonlight shining through the window. Her eyes seemed to dim as well. "How can this be?"

"That," Ash said, "no one knows. I can fill you in on the past couple of years if you'd like. That's how long I've known about Asmaria. My life story is kind of tragic."

She smiled softly. "Please," she said. "Do tell me."

And so he did. Ash told her everything. From him being abandoned by his father, the man who joined Aros and led the Forbidden against the Asmarians. The death of his mother. He told her how he learned of his abilities and struck down Rick, the event that tossed him into this world. He spared no detail, not even when reliving the details of the prior year. Ash made sure she knew of his faults.

He also told her about the Great Tree, and the more he talked, the brighter her eyes became. Reminding her of the visions she shared with him seemed to unlock more memories of her time as the Tree.

When he was done, she walked over and sat on the edge of his bed, her gleaming blade of light long vanished. "Let me see your wounds," she ordered, except, he hadn't told her about that yet.

"How did you—"

"Just show them to me," she cut him off.

He did as she told him, unwrapping the blood-kissed bandages.

"I must thank you, Ash, for sharing all that with me. You've helped me remember many things." Her hand reached toward his chest and began glowing. For a moment, Ash worried she would kill him now that he'd revealed everything to her.

As soon as her palm connected with his chest, the muscle fibers and flesh of his sternum began knitting back together. It was uncomfortable, but within a few seconds, it was over.

She released a heavy breath, slouching over slightly. Ash put his hand on her shoulder. "Are you alright?" he asked.

She smiled, "Just a little tired." Gethin stood and held her hand out to him. "Come. Let us go see the Guardians at once."

He took her hand and stood, choosing to keep the wound in his back. Let it serve as a reminder of what Kane did—as if he would need a reminder. Standing beside her, he noticed the goddess couldn't be more than five feet tall. "I'll take you straight to them."

They left the room and Ash was reminded of the guards placed outside her room. He'd forgotten about them through all the excitement. They lay prone on the floor, unconscious. "What'd you do to them?" he asked.

"Oh, they're just asleep," she replied. "They startled me when I tried to leave the chamber that held me." Ash chuckled as they strolled down the hallway.

The Guardians' estate wasn't far from the hospital; the night staff could do nothing but gawk as Ash exited the building with Gethin.

The Guardians lived in a small cul-de-sac consisting of only their homes. There wasn't much room between each house. It would have been rude to barge through their doors—which would have been all too easy—so Ash began hammering on them with the large iron knockers that each door possessed.

Gethin waited with her arms crossed and an impatient look on her face. After a couple of minutes, the first door swung open. A disgruntled-looking Avani stood in his pajamas—a long green nightshirt with a cap.

Ash couldn't stifle the laugh that burst at the sight of the man.

"What is the meaning of this?" Avani growled.

The boy stepped aside and held his hand toward Gethin,

showing the reason for the intrusion. Immediately, Avani's eyes grew wide and his jaw fell free.

"You're awake," he guffawed.

"Yes," she replied, grinning now. "It would seem as though I am."

"Please, allow me to change my clothes."

Gethin offered a slight nod, saying, "As you wish, my lord."

The door shut again and shortly after, the others began to open. Bora was also looking rather upset until Ash introduced Gethin. Leena and Dihren appeared to still be half asleep, but perked up at the sight of the Fae Queen.

They gathered at a small table in Bora's house. Ash paced the room, looking around at the decorative choices the water Guardian had made. It was, unsurprisingly, a lot of blue.

"Ash has filled me in on all that I've missed out," Gethin told them.

"How did the two of you come to be together?" Dihren asked.

"As I woke, I was drawn to the energy coming from him. I didn't know what was happening, and I was scared, so I went to him."

Leena offered, "I assume Ash has told you that Aros is back?"

She nodded solemnly. "It would seem that I did not kill the demon as I'd hoped. I thought..." she trailed off, her gaze flickering down at her twiddling fingers.

"What, madam?" Bora urged.

"I thought that I was made to defeat him. He and I are exact opposites. Aros is pure darkness, and I, light. It made sense to me then that he would perish if I pierced whatever he had in place of a heart with an object made of my light magic. However, that is not the case."

"So you don't know how to defeat him then?" Avani asked.

"I'm afraid that knowledge has not yet revealed itself to me."

"What about the obelisk?" Ash interjected. All eyes swiveled to him which made him feel as if they'd forgotten he was standing there.

"What is this obelisk?" Gethin asked.

Ash continued, "When I was taken hostage by my father, I snuck around their lair and found a throne room. Aros sat there, although, he was basically just a shadow then."

A shiver crawled up his spine as he recalled the first time he laid eyes on Aros. "There was an obelisk in the throne room as well. It was taller than me and had some sort of weird language written all over it."

"I remember seeing it on the island," Avani said. "The day he killed the remaining Forbidden. I thought it was just part of the ritual that allowed him to regain his body. He spilled Draven's blood on it." Avani shook his head briefly. "Now, it makes sense that it's being used for a different purpose. Aros didn't leave it behind; he snatched it as he flew away."

Gethin nodded and said, "That could be it. Magical objects are plentiful in this world. I wouldn't be surprised if this obelisk has multiple uses."

"That means, if we destroy the obelisk, we should be able to kill Aros for good," Ash said.

"That's as good a plan as any," Leena offered.

"Now we just need to find the both of them," Dihren said.

Bora asked, "Are any of you aware of any updates on his whereabouts via the monitors?" They all shook their heads.

"Well, we *do* have a man on the inside," Leena said.

Ash rolled his eyes. His teeth gritted when he said, "Kane isn't going to help us now. He betrayed us!"

Gethin looked at him with curious eyes. He explained as quickly as he could about Kane and what he'd done to him. Kane was the reason Ash was in the hospital in the first place.

"I may not know your friend," Gethin said, "but do not lose faith in him. When our friends and family need us most, our faith in them is sometimes all they have to cling to. Believe that he will return to us and he may do just that."

Ash took a deep breath as he nodded. *I wish for nothing more than my friend to come back,* he thought.

Enemy Lines

Kane could only pay for one room at the motel, so the following day, he lifted himself onto the roof of the building and waited for whatever Aros was sending to pick him up. He waited and waited. The sun rose, reached its apex, and then began its descent.

As the day progressed, dark clouds scattered throughout the sky, blotting out the sun. He was thankful for that. It was nearing night and a chill was creeping around the boy. A white cloud billowed out of his mouth as the temperature dropped. A screech cut through the air.

Kane jumped up from where he was sitting and searched the skies. In the distance, but closing in, was a great winged beast. A dragon.

No, as the thing grew closer, Kane noticed it was something else. Something he'd only ever read about. No one he knew had ever seen one. Like the dragons, wyverns were also of draconic blood. They used to be perceived as abominations when draconic creatures ruled the world.

"Whoa," Kane breathed out as the monster landed on the roof next to him.

The thing huffed, spraying steam and snot from its nostrils.

This wyvern was bigger than all the dragons that lived on Asmaria. The beast looked nearly identical to a dragon except for only having two hind legs.

The wyvern's scales were a charcoal gray and shimmered from the nearby streetlight. Its eyes were burning into Kane, narrow slits of flaming orange, they were like two fist-sized balls of lava amidst its scarred face. Kane wondered how old it was.

The creature crouched down, bending so that Kane could climb atop. He straddled himself around its spines as best he could and got a tight grip. Kane could fling himself on the wind with great speed, but even he was no match for a draconic beast.

"Let's go," Kane said. The wyvern craned his neck to look at Kane and a rumble issued from within. His lips parted and fangs bared. A warning.

Kane held his hands up in surrender. "Message received."

The wyvern bent his powerful legs and launched them into the air. Kane began freezing instantly. He closed his eyes and hugged his body as tightly to the wyvern as possible.

I hope this doesn't take long, he thought.

The moon was shining brightly when Kane arrived in Russia. It was difficult to see much, but even so, Kane could make out a swirling sphere of shadow. It parted as the wyvern approached and reclosed after they passed through its perimeter.

There were large fires burning all over. As they careened towards the ground, Kane noticed a multitude of figures of different shapes and sizes. Some were colossal and others not so much. The closer they got the more horrified Kane became.

It seemed as if none of the things on the ground were human. When they landed, Kane found himself surrounded by beasts he couldn't even name. The creatures growled and snarled, snapping their jaws menacingly. Claws scraped on stone and giant feet stomped around.

Kane climbed down from the wyvern's back and it launched back into the air. He fumbled for the handle of his karambit, for all the good it would do, but his fingers were too numb to get a good hold. He was freezing. He was beginning to feel the weight of his decisions, like the heaviest force of gravity pushing down on his shoulders. Why did he think this was a good idea?

Then, the sea of monsters began to part, and out waltzed the worst beast of all. He only looked slightly different from the last time he'd seen him.

His skin was still gray and he had black veins covering the parts of his body that were visible. His hair was darker than dark and his eyes were white. He was still barefoot, although, now he was dressed in a pair of white dress pants, a white dress shirt with the sleeves rolled up a bit, and a white vest.

Is he trying to make himself look less sinister? Kane wondered.

Aros walked toward him with a wicked smile on his face and his arms spread wide. "Welcome, my dear boy," he drawled. "How was the flight? Nice weather?"

Kane could feel his hatred for the demon king increase, the smile on his face only feeding the rage he was harboring. He wanted to destroy him right there. But he couldn't.

He shivered and mumbled, "It was cold."

"Yes, I supposed that would be true for you." Aros turned to one of his minions, a nasty little creature with sharp teeth and blood red eyes. Rags drooped from its body and its thick hair was braided with small bones intertwined. It wore a small dagger around its waist and had claws at the tips of its four-fingered hands.

"Bring the boy something a bit warmer to wear," he ordered. The thing ran off without a word.

"What is that thing?" Kane asked, his curiosity running wild now.

Aros grinned again. "That thing would be a goblin," he replied.

"Huh," Kane marveled. "Never knew they were real."

"There are many things that are real in this world," Aros told him. "One just needs to have the persistence to find them."

Kane wanted the small talk to be over. The goblin returned and draped a thick, black cloak over him. He brought the hood over his head and hated that he was enjoying the warmth it offered. Aros didn't deserve gratitude for anything.

"Is that better?" Aros asked. "You comfy?" Kane didn't understand why he was asking about his comfort level, but before he could answer, Aros conjured two ropes of shadow that sprang from the ground.

The tethers wrapped around Kane's wrists and retreated, bringing him to his knees. Kane bared his teeth, seething at the demon. "What is this?" he yelled. "Release me!"

"All in good time, boy," Aros replied. "First, I shall ascertain your *true* reason for being here. Are you *really* joining my side or do you wish to spy on me, to garner my secrets for the Asmarians?"

Kane had no time to reply before Aros was on him. He gripped either side of his head and a whisp of black smoke leaked from the demon's mouth and entered Kane's. His eyes fogged over and his recent memories began playing back in his mind.

Torture

Images flashed by showing Aros everything he needed to know. When it was done, the demon king let go of Kane and took a step back as the whisp of black snaked back into him. He took a shaky breath as he clapped his hands together.

"You mean to infiltrate my army," he said definitively.

"No," Kane argued. "That was a ploy to trick Ash. I swear. There can only be one winner in this war, right? Well, this way I know all my family will be safe no matter what. I'd be a moron not to take your deal." He silently begged that Aros believe him. "I only told Ash that so he'd *think* I was getting your secrets."

Aros crossed his arms. "There's really only one way to tell where your allegiance lies." He snapped his fingers and the shadows binding Kane abated. "You must do something for me to prove your loyalty."

Kane had expected as much. "What do you want?" he asked.

A devilish smile pulled at his cheeks.

Kane couldn't believe what he was preparing himself to do. Aros told him there was one other human in their midst. When

Kane asked who, the dark lord laughed heartily. Moments later, a disheveled man was dropped into the cold mud at Kane's feet.

Augustus.

Kane had wondered where Ash's father had gone off to, he just assumed Augustus was off on some other wicked business. He never expected this.

"You will torture this man," Aros told him. "It shouldn't be difficult. You no doubt harbor harsh feelings for his past transgressions, no?"

"What does torturing him accomplish?" Kane asked.

"My former accomplice has failed me too many times. I want him punished, and you, my boy, need to prove that you're willing to obey my commands. Even with as much animosity you feel for this man, torturing another man does something to the soul." A wicked grin followed the last sentence.

"Fine, I'll do it," Kane replied grimly.

Augustus turned his head slightly to look at him. Even as much as Kane despised the man, he didn't desire to inflict pain upon him so barbarically. There was no honor in it. As pointless as it seemed, if this is all it took to sway Aros' opinion, then he would do it. He had thought the demon king would require something far worse to prove himself.

"Well, what are you waiting for?" Aros asked. "Begin."

With a deep breath, Kane steeled himself for what he was about to do. The runes on his rings began to glow faintly as his hands moved to gather the winds. He felt the magic coursing through him.

Augustus was brought to his knees by the winds and he held himself there. He peered into Kane's eyes and held the gaze. Kane felt like the man could see the truth within him. He gave the slightest nod as if telling Kane that it was okay.

Kane whipped the cloak off himself; if he was going to be acting like a beast, he deserved to freeze like one.

A punch to Augustus' stomach caused him to double over, coughing. When he righted himself, Kane delivered another.

A kick to the chin.

Elbow to the nose.

Aros yawned. "I believe you've held back enough, boy. It's time to do some real damage."

Kane glared at the demon and then looked back down at his victim. A small spattering of blood decorated the whiskers around his mouth.

The mage conjured the wind to lift the man and then slammed him down, pinning him to the cold ground. The air left his lungs upon impact and he lay there, gasping for air.

Aros laughed gleefully. "Yes, that's it. More," he demanded.

Using a similar method as the one he'd used on Ash, Kane swiped a hand through the air. Blades of wind left lacerations on Augustus' forearms. Blood trickled out.

Aros licked his lips greedily at the sight of the man's blood. He showed no indication that Kane should stop, so he did it again.

At least ten slashes later, Aros held up a hand. "Okay, I think he's had enough. Let him return to the dungeon where rats like him belong."

Ash's father had crimson leaking from wounds all over his arms and back. Whimpering, he was dragged away by one of the creatures gathered there.

Kane's skin was crawling with shame. His stomach threatened to heave out anything that resided. It was freezing, and yet, he felt as if he had a fever.

"Just one more thing, Kane," Aros told him.

"Yes?"

"Kneel," he ordered.

"Kneel?"

"I am your king and you will kneel in my presence," he snarled.

Kane did as ordered, kneeling in the mud. It sounded as if some of the onlookers were laughing.

"Rise," Aros said. He turned to the same goblin who brought the cloak. "Show him to his chambers."

"Yes, Master," the thing croaked. It beckoned Kane to follow.

He retrieved his cloak and followed the goblin.

"You may call me Borg," the goblin told him. His voice was raspy and guttural, as if he had spent a lifetime growling in the shadows.

"Kane," he replied.

"I know who you are," he replied. "The dark lord has spoken of you. You are master of the winds."

"I guess that's sort of true," he admitted. "How did you find yourself working for Aros?"

The goblin spun around on him, stopping Kane in his tracks. He poked a sharp finger in his face. "You will refer to him as master, lord, or king. Understood?"

Kane was in no mood. The bile in his stomach still churned and the smell of rotten flesh from the camp did not help to improve it. He swatted the finger away. "I'll call him whatever I want. You're not in charge of me."

The goblin growled but turned back, walking faster than before. There were small shacks erected all over the place made of wood and stone. Trees were still being cleared out. It seems even the darkest of beasts prefer to live under a roof.

Finally, they came to a small hovel with the letter 'K' on the door.

"The Master will summon you when you are needed," Borg said. "Until then, stay out of our way." He trotted off as Kane entered his new home.

It wasn't much to look at. A small bedroll had been spread on the ground. There was a blanket and a bucket of water. "Well," he said to himself, "welcome home, Kane."

Friends in Low Places

Augustus was surprised to see the white-haired friend of Ash. It also worried him. Now that he knew Aros would not be making well on any of his promises, he was concerned as to what the dark lord could have persuaded the boy with to join him. He didn't think any of the Asmarians would be foolish enough to follow Aros as he had.

The veil of shadow that covered his pit had been removed, however, his way of escape was not clear. In place of the veil, there now sat a barrier made of stone and iron. The gaps in the iron rods allowed for a bit of firelight to shine through, and for that, Augustus found himself grateful.

This is what his life had come to, finding gratitude in something so simple. Sure, he could melt the iron, but Augustus knew the dark lord. Aros would have guards rotating around the pit, and if the fire mage were to try blasting his way out, he'd be swarmed before he had enough time to escape. Powerful he may be, but the numbers were against him.

Augustus scratched another tally into the wall, not daring to count them. A hushed conversation and the echoing scrape of the barrier being moved alerted him to others' presence above.

Dust glittered through the sun rays as it floated down around him. Then, it hit him. The sun shouldn't have been shining down. What is going on?

He looked up to see the silhouette of someone being lowered down into the pit with a basket in hand. It was the kid.

"Thought you might be hungry," he said, setting the basket down.

Augustus peeked inside. There was bread. Actual bread, not the moldy, filthy scraps he'd been getting. "What's going on here?" he rasped.

The boy glanced up and Augustus' gaze followed. The guards would be listening, but it looked like no one was watching for now. "I don't think we've ever formally met. Only in the times you've tried to kill us." Augustus didn't answer. "I'm Kane," he said, stretching out his hand.

Augustus ignored the offering, and instead, lifted a piece of bread from the basket and began gnawing on it.

From a pocket, Kane pulled some bandages and ointment. He whispered, "I thought you could use these."

Augustus took them warily. "What game are you playing here, kid? Trying to get me tortured some more?"

Kane sat down across from the man. "Look, I'm here to take down Aros and that's it. I feel guilty for what I did to you and that's why I brought you all this."

"He's going to find out and then you'll be right down here with me."

"I was given permission to bring you some provisions," Kane replied. "He'll never know about the other stuff."

Augustus nodded slightly as he chewed on the bread. He had forgotten how delicious non-moldy bread could be. "What's with the sun?"

Kane looked up. "What do you mean?"

"The sun never shines here," Augustus replied. "The dome of shadow keeps everything hidden."

"Oh," Kane looked confounded. "I'm not sure. When I woke up this morning, the shadows were gone. I thought it was normal. I'll have to look into it."

Augustus audibly swallowed the bite he'd been chewing. He looked at Kane with a raised eyebrow. "You really think you can betray Aros and get out of here alive?"

"I was sort of hoping you'd be able to help me with that," Kane admitted. "I didn't have a solid plan coming into this. I'm the type of person that just *does* things and figures it out as I go."

"Horrible idea, by the way."

Kane, ignoring him, said, "Now that I see you're in a predicament of your own, I figure why not work together?"

"Because the Asmarians would never trust me," he argued. "They would never believe anything I have to say."

"I wouldn't be so sure," Kane said with a smirk.

"What makes you say that?"

Kane stood to his feet, tugging on the rope twice. As it began to lift him from the pit, he said, "Gethin has broken free of the Tree."

Augustus jumped to his feet, ignoring the burning wounds on his back. He didn't know that they knew of Gethin. He only knew because of Aros. The Fae Queen has risen? What did that mean? The boy left Augustus with many questions and much to ponder.

"Where did all those shadows go that I saw last night when I arrived?" Kane asked Borg. He sort of liked the little goblin, even if he was a little crotchety.

Borg snarled, "Lord Aros only had the curtain of darkness up because he worried of peering eyes. It's been lifted because that is no longer the case."

"What do you mean?"

Borg stopped, turning around with squinted eyes. "Why all the questions, fleshling?"

"I'm part of Lord Aros' army now," he replied. "I need to know these things."

The goblin seemed to consider it for a moment and shrugged, turning back around. "The dark lord's army is nearly complete. With you, we now have an Asmarian traitor to give us all the skinny on their plans. A few more dark beasts need to be called away from their depths and the war will begin."

A flash of nervousness rifted through Kane. "Cool. Sounds like fun," he replied.

"Lord Aros requires your presence," Borg told Kane.

So far, all he'd done was lay around his hut and eat the morsels of bread that were delivered to him. His body was craving some meat, but he didn't want to appear ungrateful for what he was already getting. He knew the evil beings around the camp did not eat the same things; they could sustain themselves on much less.

"What for?" he asked Borg.

"I do not question the dark lord's orders," the goblin replied with a sneer.

"Fair enough."

Kane wrestled his shoes on and followed Borg out of the hut.

There were so many strange, menacing-looking creatures that Kane felt a pang of worry. He was concerned that the coming war would not be won without great sacrifice, although, that is the nature of war.

A lonely tower made of black stones stood in the center of the encampment. Kane hadn't seen it before.

"Is that where we're going?" Kane asked, pointing at the edifice.

"Aye," Borg replied.

There were roughly ten steps leading up to a heavy wooden door at the front of the tower. As Kane started up the stairs behind the goblin, he looked up, taking in the height of the structure. It looked to be at least fifty feet tall.

Upon entering, Kane was glad to see there were flame-lit sconces lining the walls. They walked across a long hall that was empty of any décor. Kane wasn't surprised; he didn't figure Aros to be the kind of beast to decorate his home. Once across the chamber, they entered another door that hid nothing but a spiral staircase.

Up, they began climbing. Kane was tempted to fly over the goblin's head using his wind magic but thought he'd land himself in trouble for doing so. The ascent was tiring, and when the floor finally leveled out again, Kane was breathing hard. His silent victory was that Borg was breathing just as hard.

The goblin rapped his warty knuckles on the door twice. There was no voice telling them to enter, however, the door swung open immediately. Kane saw tendrils of black curling away as they stepped into the room.

Kane's eyes began dancing around, trying to take in all that surrounded him. There were no other beings there save for

Aros and Borg. The demon king sat upon a throne of black that seemed to shift the more Kane looked at it. It was like seeing the faces of the dead trying to escape from the seat.

There were notches in the walls where oil lamps sat, flames casting a soft glow about the room. Behind Aros was the obelisk he'd had on the island; carvings of another language covered its surface.

"You wished to see me?" he asked.

"It is time we discuss your friends," Aros said simply.

"I have no friends."

Aros smirked. "Nevertheless, we shall speak of how they mean to attack."

Kane nodded, breathing in through his nose. "Of course." How was he going to pull this off? He needed to give Aros enough information so as not to seem suspicious, but also without giving away the Asmarians too much. He would have to tread carefully.

"Begin," Aros demanded.

Kane cleared his throat. "To be quite honest, My Lord," Kane put on his most trustworthy tone, "the Asmarians don't have any solid plans. None that I'm aware of, at least. I had been training the wind mages for a while, apart from trying to increase our magical abilities, they are also equipping the non-magic Asmarians with weapon training as well. They believe they will need every able body in this fight."

Aros grinned, turning to Borg. "They can be sure of that, right Borg?" He laughed and the goblin did the same.

"Yes, Lord Aros," the goblin said. "Indeed."

Something brilliant went through Kane's mind, dangerous, but brilliant all the same. A bit of information that was so useful, that even Aros would have to admit to Kane's loyalty.

"I have one more thing to share, Lord Aros," Kane said. He planted the seed and waited.

"Go on," Aros said, waving his hand.

"Something happened with the Great Tree, the one we get our magic from." He let the words simmer as the demon king leaned forward. He could see the anticipation in his eyes.

"Yes?" He licked his lips.

Even Borg's interest was piqued.

"There was a golden beacon that beamed into the sky," Kane continued. "We realized it was coming from the Tree, and when we got there, it had split open."

Aros was on his feet.

Kane went on, "Gethin has emerged, her body intact. She was still unconscious, although alive when I came here."

Aros breathed heavily through his nose. His hands curled into fists and his eyes were bulging out of his face. Kane looked to Borg; the little goblin appeared to be petrified. Kane knew he'd either just given Aros a great piece of information or made him so angry that he would kill him anyway.

The shadows seemed like they were being drawn in towards Aros. Kane took a step back and Borg was back-pedaling for the door. Aros took in two more large breaths of air and then released a blood-curdling roar.

Kane felt his emotions amplify. He knew he was rageful, but the level it increased to made him fear he would try killing anything around him. Not only the rage, but the sadness too, rose to a new level. It was as if Aros' emotions were affecting Kane's. As he screamed, spikes of shadow erupted from him in all directions. Kane and Borg narrowly dodged being impaled, however, the walls and ceiling of the tower weren't so lucky.

The structure began to crumble. Kane waited for an

opportunity, his emotions waning, and then he saw a hole in the ceiling that would allow him to escape. Borg was just within reach, and grabbing the goblin by the back of shirt collar, Kane launched into the air. They barely made it through the hole, soaring through the air.

Borg squealed as the roof of the black tower was blasted apart by Aros a second time. The beasts on the ground below were not lucky enough to avoid the falling debris. Kane heard many screeches as they were crushed by the black stones.

Aros shot into the air, his massive dark wings carrying him into the sky, wisps of smoke wafting from his body.

Kane controlled the winds as he dropped Borg. He rocketed himself below the small beast, landing first. The goblin plummeted towards the ground and Kane softened his landing at the last second.

Borg's small, beady eyes stared at Kane. The white-haired wind mage stood there smiling, hands in his pockets as if it was all too easy for him—which it was. The goblin's chest was pumping vigorously as he tried to catch his breath.

We Must Both Die

"How long has she been doing that?" Quinn asked.

Ash glanced over at Gethin who sat on a large stone near one of Asmaria's beaches. Her legs were folded and her hands rested on her knees. She held her eyes shut and had been doing so for a few days.

"At least three days," he replied. "She said she needed to meditate and hasn't budged since. She made me promise not to leave her here alone," he said with an eye roll.

"I'm sure she has her reasons." Quinn shifted nervously. "Do you know why she wants to be so close to you all the time?"

Ash thought about it for a moment. Did he detect a hint of jealousy coming from the girl?

The inclination made him smirk. "I don't know, to be honest. Although, she told me that she felt drawn to me when she woke up. Maybe it's because of the whole prophecy thing."

"Yeah," she nodded, "I'm sure that's it."

After a brief silence, Quinn continued, "I'm sorry about everything that's happened between the two of us. You know that right?"

Ash wasn't sure he was prepared to visit that topic again. He nodded and said, "I'm sorry too. We haven't been very clear with each other about our… feelings."

She chuckled, "That alone sounded weird coming from you."

Ash wasn't accustomed to talking about his feelings; he and Rick never spent much time doing that.

Quinn shuffled closer to Ash and took one of his hands. "Do you think I could make it up to you?" Ash noticed her rosy cheeks as she smiled.

He looked down at his feet and said, "I don't think it's a great idea right now. I care about you Quinn…" he trailed off.

When his eyes met hers, he saw sadness, and she let his hand fall back to his side. "But?"

"But," he continued, "I need to focus on getting rid of Aros. I think, for now, we shouldn't let our feelings get in the way of what we need to do. I can already tell this battle is going to be difficult. We're probably going to lose a lot of people, and I just can't let myself get distracted."

A tear slid down her cheek as she nodded and said, "So I'm just a distraction. Got it."

Quinn shoved past Ash, storming off the beach.

"Wait," he called out, but she marched on without another word.

Ash palmed his face, cursing himself silently. He looked back to Gethin as she remained on the large rock stoically still, silent.

A while later, as the sun began to drop again, crunching leaves alerted him to someone approaching. He'd been deep in thought, perusing his mind about the things of the past and the things yet to come.

Being startled and always expecting danger, he spun around, magic flaring to life. The purple lightning ran down his arms and sprang from his fingers in tiny arcs. He bared his teeth.

"Show yourself!" he ordered into the tree line.

With hands raised in surrender, out walked Dihren.

"Easy there, Ash," he said. "It's just me."

Ash let the magic flutter away, taking deep breaths. "Sorry, I—"

"No need for apologies," he said. "I only came to check on you two." He glanced toward Gethin, stepping in her direction.

Ash wasn't sure why, but his feet moved as if of their own volition, blocking the path to the goddess. He didn't tear his eyes away from the fire mage.

Dihren looked confused. "What are you doing? Do you think me a threat?"

Ash felt that he'd maybe hurt the man's feelings. He shook his head and relaxed, stepping aside. "I'm sorry, I don't know what's going on. I suddenly feel protective over her. I also find myself not trusting fire mages."

"I understand," Dihren said. "Between your father and Ember, I don't blame you in the slightest."

"Brandr was a good man, though," Ash replied. "I try not to think about him too much. Just makes me miss him."

Dihren nodded. "Agreed. Brandr was a mentor of mine. I only wish I had been named Guardian instead of Ember. I hate that he so easily persuaded me to think ill of you kids back then." He put a hand on Ash's shoulder. "I will never harm you or deceive you in any way, I promise."

Ash smiled. "Thank you, sir."

"Oh please, call me Dihren," he replied, waving him off. "The formalities of being a Guardian haven't kicked in for me yet. Now then," he clapped his hands together. "Do you have any updates I can take back to the group on Gethin?"

"No, she's been sitting there for days. She hasn't even so

much as twitched a muscle."

"Very well," he said, nodding. "Our Atlantean representatives await, somewhat impatiently. Alert us as soon as she comes out of this reverie."

"That won't be necessary." Ash spun around, startled by Gethin's voice. He hadn't been expecting it.

She went on, "I am ready to address my people."

Dihren bowed slightly and said, "Allow us to adjourn to the Capitol then, shall we?"

Back in the Capitol building, the seats were jam-packed full of Asmarians. Ash waited down on the main floor with Gethin, the Guardians, and three of the Atlanteans. King Gabriel had the largest smile Ash had ever seen on a person.

His arms spread wide as his voice boomed, "My old friend, it is so great to see you again!"

Gethin had smiled, saying, "Likewise, Gabriel." However, she declined to hug him, which Ash thought hurt the large man's feelings.

Along with Gabriel was his daughter, Kailani whose arms were crossed. She had dark rings under her eyes.

She must be taking Kane's running away harder than me, he thought.

Standing behind everyone, towering above them all, was Thaoc. Ash trotted over when he saw him. "Thaoc!"

"Ash," the giant replied. "Good to see you again, young man. How are you?"

"Better now that I'm up on my feet," he said.

"Yes, I am glad you've recovered. Let the things of the past stay there, eh?"

Ash smiled. "Right."

The chatter died down as soon as Gethin stepped up to address the Asmarians. She looked around, taking in the sight of everyone.

"Thank you all for coming," her voice rang out. Such a powerful voice in such a small body. "I have much to tell you regarding things that you think you know, and that which you do not. All of you have been led to believe certain things about our people, our history. Much of that which has been passed down from your ancestors ignorantly. Much of it is false; I am here to rectify that."

She paused.

Continuing, "There are things in this world that many believe to be myth. To those outside of Asmaria, they think the Fae are one of these make-believe things. However, we are many and we are powerful. Each one of you descends from the Fae folk, that is why some of you find yourself able to wield our magic.

"The magic does not pick every Asmarian simply because you are not fully blooded Fae. When I was the Tree, I was able to see each of you as you were born, and I did my best to awaken the magical nature in you all. I am sorry that it did not take for some of you."

She paused for a moment, letting the murmurs ripple through the crowd. Ash found himself confounded. He'd never imagined he could be part Fae. He just thought he was picked at random. That would never be true for him though, would it? Having been born through a prophecy.

Gethin went on, pacing the floor as she did so, "While meditating, I came to several realizations. My final attack against the demon, Aros, did not destroy him fully but reverted him to his most feeble form. It did something similar to me;

as I was dying, my body and the magic within took on the form of the Tree. This kept me alive, but only just.

"The Tree then became a chrysalis, that which grew me a new body, however, it took a long time. I nearly died from the poison I was inflicted with, but you saved me." Ash saw her gaze shift and stop on one person in the crowd. He followed her gaze and landed on Quinn. That brought a smile to his face. Then she turned and looked at Ash.

"The elixir that healed me," she continued, "I believe also sped up my metamorphosis. I fear that had none of that happened, I would not be here yet."

She looked around again, and finally said, "My last realization, and this may be the most important of all I've told you tonight. As I already told you, my magic did not destroy the demon. There is a very specific reason for that. I've shared with the Guardians that Aros and I are the opposite of one another. I am a creature of light and he is a beast of darkness."

As if for dramatic effect, Gethin held a palm up and a small orb of orange light manifested. It floated just above her palm. She pushed it up gently and it began floating upward. Ash could feel its warmth. It was different from the light blade she threatened him with; this was cozy and reminded him of happy memories. Like the time Rick showed him how to throw a proper punch. Or the time Kane got his butt kicked by Kailani.

"The reason," Gethin said, "that neither Aros nor I died that day, is because of a couple of reasons. The obelisk that he defends so aggressively is of the utmost importance. To kill him, we will first need to destroy this artifact as it harbors a piece of his retched soul. Secondly, neither of us can live while the other dies."

Gasps and whispers fluttered around the tall chamber of the Capitol building. Ash didn't understand what she was saying. He didn't understand why there were so many people with looks of horror on their faces. Even the Guardians looked shocked when he looked at them, arguing quietly between one another so that he could not hear what was said.

"Yes," she said, nodding. "In the end, Aros and I must both die."

The building exploded in a ruckus.

Goblins Aren't Evil

Kane never would have guessed that goblins were such crafty climbers or adequate builders. They'd reconstructed the tower—with help from the giants—before the sun fell. Aros had seemed to simmer down a bit and now he and Kane were sitting next to a fire along with Borg and some other creatures.

There was a thing staring daggers into Kane that almost looked like a woman. Her black hair was greasy and her eyes were dark pits on her face, glimmering in the firelight. Borg told him that she was a wraith—a creature of the dark that feasted on the blood of men.

"Tell me everything again," Aros demanded.

Kane rolled his eyes. "We've been through this, Lord Aros. I've told you everything I know."

Aros stood up and hissed, "You should have stayed until she had awoken. She could already be gathering her forces to march their way to me by now."

"Even if she is awake by now," Kane said, "you're bound to be stronger than her. She's been dormant for what, centuries?"

Aros nodded, "You're right. My mind remembers that attack she cast on me. I nearly died the last time we met. I'm more powerful now and my army is much greater than last time. I only had you feeble humans before."

That garnered laughs from all but Kane.

"My Lord," the wraith interjected, "I say we take the fight to them. Strike hard and fast now. They would never expect it." Her voice was like that of a snake.

"No," Kane said before Aros could respond. "It wouldn't work. Their defense is too well-built."

The wraith continued, "Or maybe you don't want to see your friends die." Her eyes were narrowed at Kane.

He had already proven his loyalty and now he needed to show that he was not to be trifled with. In one swift motion, he blasted a gust of wind at the creature, knocking her backward onto the ground. He was standing over her before she could recover, a karambit drawn and pressed to her throat.

He could do it. Kane would feel no remorse for ending the life of something so wicked; however, that would not serve his plans.

He growled in her face, "I have proven myself here. It would benefit you to watch how you speak to me." Then he jumped back to where he'd been sitting.

The wraith dusted herself off as she recovered back to her seat.

Aros chuckled, "Such a feisty young fellow. What would you have us do, Kane?"

Kane was taken aback. Aros wants his opinion?

"Well, I would suggest we wait here. The Asmarians built a device that shows traces of great evil in the world. It's only a matter of time before this location is discovered. We need to devise a trap of some sort for them and spring it once they're in the vicinity."

Aros nodded. "Not bad, boy."

"My Lord," Borg interrupted, "do you have any idea why the witch was unable to kill you the last time? From what I've heard, the final blow she dealt was strong enough to take out a hundred goblins."

"Are you suggesting that I am not as strong as a hundred goblins, Borg?" Aros' shadows snaked out from him, curling around Borg's neck.

Kane was unsure why he even cared but he didn't want to see the little goblin killed, especially over something so trivial.

"Lord Aros," he quipped, "I have to admit I want to hear your answer as well. I don't think Borg meant to insult you, just that if we know why Gethin's spell didn't work, we may figure out a way to ensure it doesn't happen again."

Aros smirked as he released Borg who gulped in air and clutched his throat.

"It's very simple," Aros replied. "The obelisk that I always keep near me holds a sliver of my soul, yes, I have a soul. That witch did not destroy the obelisk, only the fleshy body I had. Therefore, I was not utterly destroyed. That piece of my soul remained in the obelisk until I was able to lure the fire mage, Augustus, into my grasp."

The revelation almost made Kane leap with excitement. He now knew exactly how to kill Aros. Destroy the obelisk and his body and he'll be destroyed forever. Not only was the information pivotal to the war, but the obelisk was also within his reach. He could devise a plan that would allow him to get close enough to destroy it. He just needed to bide his time and strike at the perfect opportunity.

Kane planned to visit Ash's father again; the man may have

more information that would be useful. First, however, he needed to speak with Borg alone. Kane had a new goal since arriving, turn as many against Aros as possible. He knew he would need to be careful and tread lightly. If any of this horde of monsters turned him in, it would mean the end of his life.

The goblin was in a large tent with his head leaned back and his feet propped up. He snored lightly as Kane entered. He noted how the goblin didn't look all that different from a human.

Sure, his skin was pale and his nose and ears were abnormally pointy. His eyes were black and beady, his eyebrows thick. His long fingers ended in claws as well, but other than those things, he was just a normal guy.

Kane figured Borg had emotions and feelings, and if he were to prod them correctly, he could find an ally in the little creature.

"Psst," Kane tried to wake the beast. Borg did not stir from his slumber.

Kane walked over and placed a hand on his shoulder, shaking gently. The movement was lightning-quick. Borg rolled over and kicked the boy's feet out from under him. Kane could feel the cold steel of a dagger pressed to his throat.

The goblin breathed heavily until he realized who he was about to kill.

"Oh, it's you," he noted, releasing his hold on Kane. "Don't you know to never wake a sleeping goblin?"

Kane sat up, rubbing his throat. "Well, I certainly know that now."

The goblin sat down, sheathing his knife. "What is so important that you disturb my sleep?"

Kane chuckled softly. "I just wanted to talk to you. I've been kind of lonely since I got here and you've been kind to me."

The goblin shook his head. "What, you think we're friends? Goblins have no friends!"

Kane scoffed, "That can't be true. You're a perfectly likable guy."

Borg wagged a finger in Kane's face. "Do *not* call me 'guy'."

Kane held his hands up. "Okay, fine. Just tell me about your life. I want to know more about where you come from, your family, your hobbies."

The goblin cleared his throat, seeming to relax a little. "There's not much to tell. We goblins tend to dwell in caves and anything else that runs beneath the ground. I was the leader of my clan before all of this."

Kane was surprised to hear they were sophisticated enough to develop clans.

"Where is your clan now?"

There it is, the emotion Kane was looking for. Borg didn't make a sound but the pain was written on his face.

"They're dead," Borg said. "Killed by Lord Aros."

"How could you serve him after what he did to your clan?" Kane didn't mean it as an accusation but felt that it may have come off that way. He added, "I mean no disrespect in asking that."

He waved his hand before agreeing, "You're right. I should have followed him. I originally told him no, but then, he began slaughtering my family. When the blade was held to my neck, I said yes. I'm a coward if you want to know the truth. I saw no other way out but to agree to his terms."

Kane gently placed a hand on the goblin's shoulder. "I'm sorry all that happened to you. Do you think you'd ever defy Aros if given the chance?"

Borg seemed to think about it, then said, "I'd like to think I'd be brave enough to stand against him. But…" he paused, then, "I will never know for sure unless it happens."

Kane nodded his hand. Borg wiped his face and asked, "What about you? Why did you join forces with the demon king?"

This could be his chance to sway the goblin's mind, to have him oppose Aros. Kane whispered, "I'm here to take him down from the inside." Then he grinned.

The goblin looked surprised. "But, I watched you torture the man. You were ruthless. You enjoyed it."

Kane nodded solemnly. "I knew I would have to do certain things to gain his trust, and Augustus has caused so much pain to my friends and I, that I wanted to hurt him. It being him made things easier. Still, I'm not proud of what I did."

"I see," Borg said. "Then why did you save me in the tower? I'm just a nasty little goblin."

"No," Kane began to argue, "you're more than that. I've been able to see it from the start. And now, the way you talked about your clan, I can see there is more to you than just being a goblin. You care a lot about those you consider family. I don't expect you to think me of me as a brother or anything like that, but maybe a friend."

Kane offered his best winning smile. The goblin returned it, revealing his jagged teeth.

The goblin's eyes darted to the tent opening and Kane's followed. The flap swung shut. Someone had heard them.

Kane flew from the tent and looked around. There were too many creatures milling about to see who had eavesdropped. Borg came out shortly, sniffing the tent flap.

"Wraith," was all he said.

Kane launched himself into the air and searched for a wraith frantically. Then he found her. Nichella, the wraith from the previous night, was sprinting away from the tent. She was headed for Aros' tower. Kane refused to let her reach it.

He was on her in seconds, scooping her up with wind and spiriting her flailing body away. Finally, he found an empty spot where no other creatures scrambling around. The wind mage dropped them down, the wraith falling hard into the dirt. He hoped with all he had that none of the others had seen him steal away with the wraith.

She rolled to her feet and snarled, "Lord Aros will have your head for this. And the goblin's too."

"He'll never find out," Kane retorted.

"Traitor!" she spat. She flexed her hands and ten-inch spikes sprang from her wrists. "I'll end you here and now!"

Kane pulled his karambit out. "Let's see you try."

She needed no other invitation. Nichella sprang forth, stabbing at him wildly. He ducked and dodged every spiked jab she threw at him. Kane knew from the way she was fighting that she'd never had any formal lessons. She was just a crude animal that needed culling, and he would oblige.

He caught one of her arms and then the other, shoving the spikes into her stomach. She grimaced and gasped as blood leaked from her wounds. Kane knew he could not let her live after hearing what he and Borg had discussed, however, he wasn't cruel.

Making it as quick and painless as possible, Kane swiped his karambit and removed the wraith's head from her body. He cleaned his blade quickly and left, heading back to Borg's tent to tell him what happened. Even though she wasn't human, Kane still felt sick.

Unlock the Power

"My Lady, surely you're mistaken," Bora argued with Gethin.

All the Asmarians had been dismissed after chaos erupted at the revelation their goddess had shared with them. Ash found himself unable to close his mouth as his jaw dropped upon hearing the news.

"I am not," she replied. "Believe me, I wish there was another way. I do not wish to die, however, I will do what I must to protect this world. Aros is a being that must be destroyed at all costs, and if I am to pay the ultimate price, so be it."

"There has to be another way!" Ash cried out.

All the time he'd spent with Gethin had allowed him to grow closer to her. He'd never had a motherly figure in his life and she was the closest he was going to get.

"I understand this may be hard for all of you," Gethin went on, "but you must realize that it's the only way. I would not say it if it were not so."

"What if we were to destroy the obelisk and Aros?" Leena asked.

"A piece of his soul would attach to something else," Gethin answered. "That is how he works. He is an aberration, an anomaly in the world that must be weeded out. Aros is a plague upon the Earth."

"What I don't get," Avani broke in, "is why all of this is happening *now.* I mean, he only surfaced a thousand years ago, the first time you fought him, right? Where was he before that?"

"History is often written to benefit the writer, rather than being completely truthful," Gethin told them. "Aros is a thing that has been around so long that no one can pinpoint his origin. However, his evil has not always been this great. I would venture that many have fought him in times past and lost, but he could not be killed because those who tried did not have the tools to do so.

"Everything that you believe to be a myth is real. Mankind has been led to believe the gods of old are nothing more than mythology, but they are very real, or at least they used to exist. Every creature that you can fathom has existed in one part of time or another, in one realm or another. The world has undergone many eras of darkness and there was always a hero who thwarted the demon's plans, just as there is now."

Ash shook his head. "I can't believe it. So, we have to let Aros kill you? What is the point of that? Where is the justice in that?" His face was hot.

She smiled sadly. "No, child. We will work together to destroy Aros' obelisk and his body. Then, I will take my own life. The justice is that he will cease to live."

Ash couldn't listen any further; he stormed out, unsure of where he was going. Shouts of his comrades tried to halt him, but he would not slow. He ran, letting his feet pick his path, and found himself atop Sunset Crest. The view wasn't as beautiful at night, however, the moon shone in all its glory.

He laid down and closed his eyes, wishing all the thoughts would flutter away. Soon enough he drifted to sleep.

The warm sun prickled his eyelids, waking him from his sleep. He began walking home, conjuring lightning as he did, letting it arc around his fingertips.

Will we still have magic after she's gone? he wondered.

"There you are," Rick said, a look of concern on his face. "I heard you ran off. Thought you might have gone to join Raimir already."

He shook his head. "Nah, I'm not ready for that yet. I was just… upset."

"Feel like talking about it?"

Ash told him everything that was bothering him and when he was done, Rick said, "Life isn't forever, son. I think what Gethin plans to do is very brave. I also think that you, and any of your friends, would do the same to protect the world. We can't harbor bad feelings toward Gethin for choosing this."

Ash nodded his head. "You're right." He paused and then said, "Being on this island has made you smart."

Rick grabbed him, putting him into a headlock. "Always the smarty pants, huh?"

They laughed as they wrestled around with each other.

Later that day while Ash was working on summoning his magic, Gethin approached.

"What are you doing?" she asked.

"I need to get stronger so that I can join Raimir," he replied.

"Can I help?"

"Sure," he said, "I can always use some tips."

Ash sat with his legs crossed and Gethin walked around in front of him, sitting down and crossing her legs as well. "Close your eyes," she ordered.

He did. He felt her hand touch his head and it was like being electrocuted with positive energy. All the soreness and fatigue from training went away. He felt as if he could do anything.

"Dig deep," she told him. "There is a well of magic within you greater than any mage alive. Find it."

He searched within himself, retreating into his mind a bit. "What should I be looking for?" His voice sounded far away to his ears.

"It looks different for everyone," she replied, "but you'll know it when you see it. Search your soul, Ash."

It was like picking his way through blankets of darkness, and then finally, a spark. The faintest flicker of purple caught his mind's eye. He dragged himself through the murk, inching closer.

"I see it," he said, marveling at the sight. Amidst the darkness was an orb of amethyst lightning. It stretched out feebly in all directions, like a withering spiderweb.

"Describe it."

He told her exactly what he was looking at and when he finished, she said, "Your magic is being blocked. It's not flowing through you completely."

"How do I unblock it?"

"Go to it, grab hold, and don't let go until I tell you."

Ash began moving closer. The orb was roughly the size of a basketball now that he was so close. His hands looked blurry as he reached out. When they connected with the magic, his body went rigid and he let loose a cry of pain.

"That's it!" Gethin shouted. "Don't let go! Just a little longer!"

The searing pain intensified as chambers began to open

within the orb. The lightning began spreading and spreading. The spiderwebbing magnified in a glorious display of color.

"You can let go now," Gethin said.

When he released the magic, it was like sinking into a cold pool of water. He opened his eyes as Gethin removed her hand from his head. She had a wide smile on her face. He wanted nothing more than to collapse.

"Try your magic now," she said.

Ash opened his palm, conjuring the magic. Lightning formed instantly, however, it was different than before. It wasn't erratic and difficult to control. It was calm, almost like a liquid. It would take any shape he could imagine, switching between knives, swords, and spears. He imagined a shield forming around his left arm and it was so.

He reached for the Atlantean bow and with a snap, it appeared in his hand. He pulled the string taut and a deep purple arrow of lightning materialized.

"It's different from before," Ash said. "It feels so much more powerful."

He released the arrow. The missile flew and landed true on the metal target he'd been aiming at. Normally, any lighting he flung at the metal targets would result in a loud bang and a shower of sparks. This time, however, the arrow went straight through.

An orange-glowing hole appeared in the metal and the electrified arrow hit the ground behind it, causing the grass to catch fire. The nearby mages turned to gawk at him before a water mage put out the fire, shaking his head.

"Magic is a beautiful thing," Gethin said.

Ash couldn't contain his excitement. He was ready to join Raimir and begin his training in the foreign realm.

"Are you sure there's no other way to defeat Aros?" he asked.

"I am sure. You needn't worry over me, Ash. I have lived a long life, longer than any man ever will. The universe has given much to me, and now it's time that I return the favor.

He nodded, resigned. "Then there's only one other thing I need to do," he replied. "It's time to tell the Guardians that I'm ready to join Raimir. If you're going to sacrifice yourself to protect the world, then the least I can do is make sure you have to fight Aros as little as possible."

Ash was glad to have Gethin behind him; the Guardians had yet to give him an answer as to whether they would allow him to leave or not.

"I'm ready to join Raimir," he told them.

None of them reacted at first, then Avani sighed. "What do you think of this, Lady Gethin?"

She sounded positively upbeat. "Ash has my full support. I've conversed with Raimir a time or two, as well as others from his realm, and they are terrifying entities, although good at heart. They will do right by him. I believe he will rival the four of you when he returns."

Avani scoffed at that. "I guess we'll just have to have ourselves a little duel when you get back then."

Ash smiled. "So you're all okay with me going?"

Leena interjected, "We know that you would go either way. This way, we don't have to give you any more punishments. It's exhausting!"

He laughed, rubbing his neck nervously. "Sorry about that."

"Never mind," she said, waving her hand. "Just be safe and try not to worry about all of us too much."

They left and Ash bid Gethin farewell. He needed to go tell

Rick and gather some things for his journey. He wanted to tell Quinn, but the desire to get out of there and be with Raimir again outweighed that. She would be okay without him.

After Rick was informed and his bag was ready, Ash reached out with his mind.

Raimir, he called out. *I'm ready.*

There was no response, save for the loud crack of thunder and the flash of lightning. A shape appeared and Ash's smile reached his eyes. As Raimir grew closer, he became confused. Was this not his friend? The bird was bigger than he remembered Raimir being, and instead of looking like a regular giant falcon, this bird was covered in black feathers. The wind whipped Ash's hair as the bird landed.

Death of the Wraith

A ros walked up to Kane with the head of the wraith in his hand. He held it out so that Kane and the head were face to face. The white-haired boy wanted to hurl the meager contents within his stomach.

"I want to know who has killed her," Aros said. "And I want to know now."

"How should I know who it was?" Kane asked indignantly.

A black scythe appeared and the blade was on Kane's neck before he could react. "Tell me the truth," Aros ordered.

Before Kane could respond, Borg stepped forward. "It was me, My Lord. I killed her. I caught her stealing from me, and when I confronted her, she attacked. I defended myself."

The scythe vanished and aros leaned down to study the goblin. Kane looked between the two nervously, and then Aros began laughing, tossing the wraith's head into the dirt.

"You goblins are such a rambunctious bunch, aren't you?" he continued laughing.

"Yes, Sire," Borg replied with a bow.

"Feed what's left to the serapentis," Aros said as he turned and began walking away.

The serapentis were so nasty that they had to be held at bay by a cage made of shadow. There were ten of them cramped in a tight space, snarling and snapping their fanged jaws at anything that walked by. Their snake-like bodies slithered around and their two front legs jutted out with clawed toes.

The eyes unsettled Kane the most; black pits with rivers of red separating the pitch like snake eyes.

The beasts devoured the body of the wraith within seconds.

"Well, now what?" Kane asked.

"You're the one with all the bright ideas," Borg retorted.

"That's true." He looked around to ensure there were no prying ears, and then, leaning in, he whispered, "I need to see Augustus again."

Borg had sent the two imps who'd been guarding the pit away so that Kane could sneak down and converse with Augustus. Same as last time, Kane delivered to the man some provisions to hold him over for a little while.

"Before you say anything," Augustus began, "I demand you tell me everything there is to know about Gethin. How is it that she has risen?"

"Man," Kane said as his feet touched down, "Firing off the questions already?"

"I *need* to know," he pleaded, eyes locked on Kane.

"Okay," Kane said, running fingers through his hair. "Just try not to be too disappointed though, because I don't know very much."

Kane thought it best to start with everything that had happened since Aros nearly destroyed the Great Tree with his and Ash's combined power. He spared no detail, recounting everything he could remember. He told Augustus of the

Atlanteans and the elixir they created that healed the Tree.

Kane finished with telling him of the golden beacon that blasted into the sky and how, when everyone gathered around the Tree, they found the physical embodiment of her lying on the ground.

When he finally stopped talking, the man's mouth hung open. He shook the shock away and began eating the bread Kane brought.

"I can't believe it," he said with a mouthful. "I've been racking my brain with possibilities since your previous visit, and part of me didn't even believe you."

"You've been out of the loop in Asmaria for a long time. I say, it's a ripe time to get you back in."

Augustus shook his head slightly. His eyes looked scared. "I don't know. I'm worried they'll take one look at me and throw me in prison. Or worse."

Kane's eyebrows furled. "It won't be any worse than this," he gestured around the pit. "I mean, I've been in an Asmarian prison. It's not that bad and, at least there you'll be home."

"Home," Augustus repeated.

In the dim light, Kane could see a lonely tear trickle down his scruffy face.

"I've not had one of those for such a long time. How could I have been such a fool?" Then he began to weep.

Kane didn't know what to do or say so he just laid a supportive hand on the man's shoulder.

Wiping his face, he said through the sobs, "You must think I'm pathetic. I wouldn't blame you. I *am* pathetic."

"Look," Kane replied, "I'm not particularly good in situations like this, but, you're not pathetic. You've been lost. Aros tempted me before I came here, that's how I knew he would accept me. He wanted me here. I know how hard it is to say no to the things he can offer. You've done some pretty horrible things, I won't deny that. But you need to see that I'm offering you a second chance, a chance to make things right with Asmaria, and with Ash."

He looked up at Ash's name. "Do you think he would ever forgive me for the things I've done?"

Kane sighed. "I don't want to give you false hope by saying yes but Ash is a good kid. He's very kind and loyal to his friends. I think there's a good chance he'll forgive you, but I know it'll take time. And if he doesn't, you don't get to hold it against him."

Augustus nodded, clearing his throat. "So, what's our next move?"

"I need to destroy that obelisk," he said. "Aros told me that it's what kept him alive the last time Gethin beat him."

"That's not going to be as easy as you think."

"What do you mean?"

"The obelisk can't be destroyed by any normal means," he said. "Of all the time that Aros has spent in my head, I've never been able to gather that information. It won't be as simple as blasting apart a rock. It's going to take a significant amount of power to destroy it, and I doubt you'll find the means here."

Kane wrung his hands together as he thought about what he could use. "Is there anyone here that would know how to destroy it besides Aros?"

Augustus thought about it. "I don't think so."

"I'll ask Borg."

"Oh, not the goblin," Augustus looked disgusted. "What a vile creature."

Kane looked at him incredulously and said, "As if you're not a vile creature?"

"Fair enough," he chuckled.

"Borg just so happens to want to take Aros down too, by the way, so when we bust out of here we have to take him with us."

"You're the wind mage. Can you carry such a heavy load?"

Kane smiled knowingly. His means of arriving to this land were different from how he intended to leave it. He reached into his boot and pulled free the small silver whistle that would call a dragon from Asmaria.

"Is that—", Augustus began.

"A dragon whistle. It'll take some time for it to reach us so the timing has to be perfect when we make our escape. I'm just hoping Aros can't hear it as well."

"He said he doesn't know how to destroy it, eh?" Borg asked after Kane told him everything he and Augustus discussed.

"We're going to have to take it back to Asmaria with us."

"How do you plan to get back?"

"Dragons."

"Oh no," Borg said, shaking his head frantically. "Goblins do *not* do well in the air."

"You're just going to have to get over your fear of heights," Kane retorted. "It's the only way. Aros isn't going to just let us walk out of here. It's going to be a fight trying to escape, especially after we steal the obelisk."

"At least we know where he keeps it," Borg said.

"I just hope my wind is strong enough to carry it."

"Don't you worry," Borg said rather chipperly. "We goblins are very stout for creatures of such a short stature. I'm sure I can heft it if need be." He flexed his grey bicep for effect.

"Excellent," Kane said, mulling over a plan that would most certainly get them killed if it were to fail.

Return of Raimir

Ash was in a defensive stance, preparing himself to fight if this giant black bird wanted to attack.

"Who are you?" he yelled up at it.

He wasn't sure, but it almost looked like the bird was smiling.

I know, Raimir's voice echoed around in his head, *I look a bit different.*

Is that really you?

Of course. It would seem that both of us have undergone some changes since we last met. The healers in my realm say that my injuries opened the path for me to grow more than expected.

Ash nodded. *So, you should be thanking me, then?*

Let's not get ahead of ourselves.

Ash laughed, then said out loud, "Are you ready to get out of here?

Raimir leaned down so Ash could climb onto his back. *Let's go. The sooner we get there, the sooner your training can begin.*

Ash climbed onto his dark back and grabbed two fistfuls of feathers, excitement running through him. He yelled with a *whoop* as Raimir bent his legs and they launched into the air.

The wind roared in his ears as Raimir said, *Ready yourself.*

Ash dug his hands in better and squeezed his knees tighter.

With the sound of thunder exploding into Ash's ears, he saw a brief flash of lightning before the world around him was whisked away.

An immense pressure closed around his whole body and he could feel nothing else. Total darkness with random flashes of light flying by was all Ash could see. He tried looking around but it was as if his body had been turned into energy. It was confounding.

How long it lasted, he did not know, but when his body took shape again under the massive beast, the world had changed.

Ash took in gulps of air and looked around. They were no longer flying over an ocean but rather a vast land of hills, trees, and mountains. It was breathtaking. Two suns shone brightly amidst an icy blue sky with scant clouds.

Where are we? he transmitted to Raimir.

Tuvetal, came the reply. *A world where creatures buried in mysticism reside. Never before has a human set foot in this realm. It will be most... interesting.*

Ash wasn't entirely certain he liked the sound of that.

Upon further investigation, Ash came to realize just how expansive Tuvetal was. The trees below must have been hundreds of feet tall. The mountains were larger than any he could have imagined. There were lakes and rivers that stretched for miles. Suddenly, the size of Raimir made a lot of sense.

I must warn you, Raimir interrupted his thoughts, *not all beasts in my world are intelligent. Not all of them will care for your well-being. You must guard yourself well.*

Won't you be with me the whole time?

No. There are some things you must do alone, he replied. *Your training has officially begun, which brings me to the more difficult part of this. I will ask that you forgive me for what you shall endure. It is not my intention to let harm befall you, however, through fire, you will be born anew.*

Ash's face contorted with confusion and he shook his head. *Raimir, what are you talking about?*

Do you see the palace in the North?

Ash looked to see a palace reaching toward the sky in the distance. It sat just before a range of mountains with white tips.

I see it.

That is your destination. Raimir's body suddenly turned towards the ground. They dove and several times Ash almost lost his grip on the bird.

After leveling back out, Raimir was navigating through the massive trees with expert precision.

You must find your way to the palace. Do whatever it takes to survive.

Before Ash could form a response, Raimir flipped over, flying upside down. Ash tried to hold on but it was no use. It only took a few seconds before his fingers slipped on the downy feathers of the giant bird and the boy began falling toward the forest floor.

He fell at least twelve feet and never knew he could be so grateful for mud. Ash rolled as his feet hit the sticky goop. The impact of the tumble caused the wound in his back to throb.

"Raimir!" he yelled as the bird swooped high above the trees and vanished from sight. "Dumb bird," he mumbled as he began clawing his way through the mud, breathing hard. Small scrapes decorated his arms from the fall.

The pit of mud was large and it took him several minutes to navigate himself to dry ground. The sounds of the jungle surrounded him. Chirruping birds and calls from a myriad of beasts let him know that he was not alone. He looked up. Raimir told him he had to get to the palace in the North. The treetops would provide a better vantage point and allow him to get his bearings.

There was a tree nearby with low-hanging branches. He gripped the lowest one and began to climb, however, the mud caking his shoes wouldn't allow him to grip properly.

He let out a deep sigh. "Guess I need to find some water first," he said.

Ash marched on through the dense trees, an eerie feeling crawling across his skin as if he were being watched. The magical energy flowed just beneath the surface and would form in an instant.

The mud continued to harden as Ash searched for a water source. He guessed that it took him about twenty minutes before finally finding a murky pond. Nothing had jumped out at him yet and the feeling of not being alone had fled. He didn't realize how hot he'd become until the soothing water quenched his thirsty skin.

Ash scrubbed furiously at the mud on his shoes and clothes.

A ripple.

The water was disturbed on the far side of the pond. Ash began to creep backward from the water. Something large was moving towards him.

It disturbed his mind.

Who dares into my lair? a whisper of a deep voice asked. The hair on his arms prickled.

Ash didn't answer but continued backing away. When his

feet were on dry land again, he summoned the magic into his hands. Purple spheres of lightning formed in his palms as they rested at his sides.

Answer me! the voice roared in his head. It felt like his brain was vibrating off his skull. The spheres vanished as he clutched the sides of his head, falling to a knee.

The water broke apart as the largest snake Ash had ever seen began slithering out. The massive beast was the same swirl of brown and green as the water from which it came.

My, what have we here? King Dolgotha has sent me a hairless ape as a snack.

Ash finally replied. *Stay away from me.*

But you have so willingly entered my waters. It would go against my honor if I allow you to leave now.

"Screw this," Ash said aloud. Lighting sparked to life around his hands and he took a defensive stance. "I don't have time for this, so if you want to kill me, then go ahead and try."

Sword in the Stone

Quinn knew that Ash would be leaving to join Raimir's realm, but the news that he'd already left still hit her like a punch to the gut. She'd expected more time before he had to leave, or at the very least, that he would have said goodbye.

She tried not to harbor any negative feelings toward him, realizing that he didn't owe her anything.

The beaches of Asmaria had always been a happy place for Quinn, and after spending time with Ash there, they were even more so. She stood there on the North Beach where they had walked in the shallow water, commanding the water around her. Conjuring water from nothing always took more energy than manipulating what already existed.

The water swirled around her, forming into spheres, rising and falling. She whisked a waver into her palm and held it up, turning it into ice and then back to liquid.

Water began to shift near her, but it wasn't her doing it. She peered down as bubbles formed letters.

Come see me.

She smiled. Leena sometimes sent messages like that. It was easier than having someone run a message to the recipient but it only worked when the sender knew exactly where the message needed to go. Leena just had this uncanny way of knowing where her fellow water mages happened to be.

As Quinn walked back through the jungle, she waved her hand and the water receded from her clothes. She was dry again.

The Guardians were standing with Gethin at the fountain in the center of town. She thought how silly it was now that she had met the man it was modeled after.

The Guardians waved to her as she approached. Their expressions were impossible to read but Gethin wore a smile. Quinn thought how beautiful she was with her auburn hair spilling over her shoulders.

"You wanted to see me?" she asked the group.

"Yes," Leena replied with a nod. "Well, *actually,* Lady Gethin asked for an audience with you."

"Oh?"

Gethin looked at Leena and back to Quinn. "Walk with me, child."

The two walked down the street. Quinn looked over her shoulder to find befuddled looks on the Guardians' faces.

"You have sadness in you," Gethin said, catching Quinn off guard.

"Um," she began, fumbling for the words.

"It's okay. I know you worry for Ash. Let your heart be at ease, child; he will be alright."

Quinn was relieved to hear that. "Thank you for the reassurance."

"I have a task for you," she continued. Quinn didn't respond and Gethin went on. "There are many things unfolding as we speak. The Asmarians are growing stronger but it will not be enough to defeat Aros. Not totally anyway. Something more powerful is needed."

A flash of fear went through Quinn.

Gethin went on, "You know that I must die in the end to destroy Aros."

Quinn nodded.

"There is more that we will need to defeat him. Aros has an obelisk that harbors a portion of his soul. It is a powerful magical artifact and only another artifact of greater power can destroy it. This is where your assistance is required."

"Me?" she asked. "How do you mean?"

She stopped and waited for Quinn to turn and look at her. "You've heard tale of a magical sword. The sword in the stone?"

Quinn thought back and a faint memory surfaced. The sword in the stone was a story about a king who liberated the blade from its rocky prison. He pulled it free and saved his kingdom with its magic. The myth wasn't as popular in Asmaria as it was in other parts of the world.

"I vaguely remember the story."

"This sword is real. It's the Sword of Pescilon. Many have known it as the Bane of Darkness. I believe it to be the one item that can destroy the obelisk."

"Lady Gethin," Quinn said, shaking her head and wringing her hands. "Why are you telling me all this?"

"Dear Quinn," she replied with a smile. "I want you to retrieve the sword. Bring it back and we may have a hope of defeating the demon king for good."

Quinn hadn't left the island in a long time and she didn't know the first place to look. A question burned inside her. "Why me?"

"Call it my intuition telling me that you'll be the perfect

mage to send on this quest, although…" she trailed off.

"Although what?" Was Gethin second-guessing her decision?

"I also have a feeling this quest will require two."

"Who shall I take with me?"

"I will leave that up to you," she said. "Don't think on it too long, though. You need to leave in three days."

Gethin left her there to mull over the quest presented to her. Who would she pick to go with her? Her brain was telling her to pick one of the Guardians or another capable adult. Something else was telling her to go in a different direction. She wouldn't need the full three days to decide. Quinn's feet carried her back to the beach, knowing before she knew in her mind who she would take.

It's All About Water

Being a strong water mage, Quinn was able to visit the new kingdom of Atlantis whenever she liked. However, the sentries standing guard almost always gave her fits. For some reason, they still weren't accustomed to outsiders showing up unannounced.

She stood at the precipice of the great underwater city with spears lowered into her face. Quinn had told them she was there to see Kailani and they sent for the princess right away.

After a few minutes, she walked down the steps to where Quinn waited. The princess didn't look very happy to see the mage.

"Yes?" she asked, folding her arms across her chest.

Quinn cleared her throat. "Are we able to go speak somewhere more private?"

"Of course," she replied with a fake smile.

Kailani marched over to Quinn, grabbing her by the wrist. They launched through the water, moving faster than Quinn would have been able to on her own. They breached the water and walked onto the dry beach.

"Are you okay?" Quinn asked, beginning to worry for the girl.

"I'm fine," she said curtly. Quinn didn't believe her. "What do you want to talk about?"

"Lady Gethin has assigned me a mission," she began, "and I want you to go with me."

Kailani's face seemed to soften then. Her creased brows eased a bit. "What kind of mission?"

"Lady Gethin has figured out that the obelisk Aros keeps close is one of the artifacts that keeps him alive. We have to destroy it. She says we need an equally powerful weapon to do so."

"And we can help with that?"

Quinn nodded. "There is a magical sword somewhere that she wants us to retrieve. She says it'll do the trick."

Kailani considered it for a moment. She looked into Quinn's eyes. "Why do you choose me to come with you?"

Quinn hadn't given it much thought. "I'm not sure," she said honestly. "Gethin told me I would need one other person for this journey and your name was the first that entered my mind. Call it a gut feeling?"

"Very well."

"So, you'll go?"

Kailani smiled genuinely then. "I'll go."

"That's great!" Quinn moved to hug the girl but thought better of it. They were friends but they hadn't the opportunity to grow that close.

"Did Lady Gethin happen to mention where we will find this sword?"

Quinn thought back. Her lips pursed. "No. We'll need to see if we can get that information out of her. She may not even know where it is. Gethin said we have three days to prepare before we need to leave."

"I'll have to speak with my father," she said. "I'll meet you at the fountain in the next couple of days. That should give us enough time to gather some gear and allow Gethin to tell us of the sword's whereabouts."

"Agreed," Quinn said. "See you then."

The basilisk struck at Ash with great speed. Ash was faster. He dodged, lashing out his hand which sent bolts of purple arcing into the beast. The thing roared in Ash's head but it didn't appear to be injured.

The snake shook its head as if water was stuck in its ear. *You'll pay for that,* it hissed.

The snake lunged again, causing Ash to dodge the same as before. He noticed too late that it was a feign. The snake's tail had creeped out of the water and swept Ash off his feet. The air left his lungs in a loud huff.

Two rows of massive fangs were rocketing toward him. Ash rolled away just in time, the snake clashing with the ground.

"Look," Ash started. "You don't have to do this. Just let me go!"

I cannot, Ape. I claim you as my dinner.

It seemed like the snake was not going to give up.

Ash conjured the Atlantean bow into his hand. He pulled the string back and an amethyst arrow of lightning materialized. He could hear the hum in his ears, feel the vibrating energy along his cheek. He waited.

The snake struck again with its jaws as wide as they could go. Ash released the arrow. Fast as lightning, the bolt zipped through the air and into the creature's mouth. The mouth snapped shut and the snake paused, then suddenly, it dropped. The great beast's head and body slammed into the ground.

Ash could see a cauterized hole atop the snakes head. His arrow had pierced through the roof of the snake's mouth and exited the other side. Ash sat down roughly, his body worn from the brief encounter.

He noticed that his hands and legs were trembling. Whether it was from fear or adrenaline, he would have to wait for the latter to wear off to find out.

After resting for a bit, Ash cleaned himself the rest of the way off, scrubbing the dried bits of mud away from his shoes and fingers. When he was finished, he noticed how dim the forest was becoming. A sense of unease came onto him as the sounds of the jungle began to increase.

Ash desperately scrambled around, gathering as much kindling and firewood as possible. He made a small pile, remembering something he watched on TV many years ago.

With a finger, he began releasing a small amount of lightning. As powerful as his magic was, he didn't want to obliterate his kindling. He wanted to conjure just enough to create a small flame. A candle flame began licking at the dry leaves and small sticks.

Ash began blowing on the flame gently as he placed a few larger pieces around it. Within a couple of minutes, he had a large fire going. Ash found himself extremely grateful for the heat of the flame. He sat with his back against the trunk of one of the colossal trees, hoping with everything that this world didn't have oversized mosquitos.

World of Giants

Ash wasn't entirely sure what to expect on his first night in a foreign realm filled with beasts vastly larger than those of his world, although, it didn't come as much of a surprise when he found himself forever chasing sleep which outpaced him. He was only able to doze off a few times before the hints of sunrise teased him from above.

At least his clothes had dried in the warm night air, giving him a silver lining if there was one to be had.

The sky had gotten brighter more quickly than it would have on Earth, no doubt due to the double suns of this world.

Ash slugged to his feet, wanting to get started as quickly as possible. The sooner all of it was over, the sooner he could go back home.

He pondered that word as he reached for a low-hanging branch of the tree he'd leaned against all night. Home. First, he was reminded of the apartment in New York. Only then did he realize how much he'd taken it for granted, how selfish he was back then.

Then, he began thinking of the new home he shared with Rick on Asmaria. When he thought about the times they'd spent having dinner together and laughing with each other, he couldn't help but smile. There didn't seem to be any other place he'd rather be.

Around halfway up the tree Ash had to stop for a break. Even as physically fit as he was, the amount of climbing he'd done left him breathing hard. The branch he sat on was roughly five feet wide which gave him plenty of room to sprawl without worrying about falling. Glancing over the edge, Ash realized how high he was and a flutter of fear hit him. If he fell from that height, he'd die.

After resting for a few minutes and wiping at the sweat that had gathered along his brow, he began climbing again. He was lucky the branches were close enough together to allow him to reach them easily; it was only slightly more difficult than climbing stairs.

Throughout all of this, the feeling of being watched never left him. The sounds of the forest were a melody of terror in his ears, not knowing what waited for him. Ash had the uncanny feeling that everything is this world was yearning to kill him.

He couldn't think about things like that, not yet at least. He needed to get his eyes on that temple.

Finally reaching the top, Ash breathed hard as sweat dripped down the sides of his face and trickled down his spine. He stood at the apex of the gargantuan tree, gazing at the beauty before him. The suns were nearing midday, white wispy clouds strolled by as a slight breeze ruffled the tops of the trees and Ash's hair. He welcomed it.

Without something trying to end his life, he was able to marvel at the beauty of Raimir's realm. Tuvetal was like something from a dream, or nightmare.

Ash scanned the expanse of forest and found the temple. It

was so far away. He was worried he would have to climb one of these trees every couple of days just to get his bearings.

Back on the ground, Ash felt like throttling Raimir for doing this to him. His arms and legs already felt like jelly and he hadn't even began trekking yet. He pulled a waterskin from his bag and took a deep drink. He'd need to find some fresh water soon, preferably some that did not have a ravenous snake dwelling within it.

Sure of which way to walk, he took off again, walking as quickly as possible. Ash was thankful that this part of the forest wasn't dense with small underbrush. That would have made it a nightmare to navigate through. With the trees as large as they were, it was like walking around the streets of New York, which he had only done twice.

After hiking for a while, Ash was beginning to feel some energy seep back into his body. He decided to play with magic, twirling lightning through his fingers. He practiced making different shapes.

A shield.

A javelin.

A dagger.

It came much easier to him since Gethin showed him how to unblock his magic.

Based on the dimness of the light around him, Ash noted that the suns were nearing the horizon. He would need to stop and make camp soon. The sound of trickling water hit his ears. He stopped, listening. Then, he began walking faster toward the sound.

A creek.

Ash had never been so excited to see a creek before. He

looked around it first, checking for anything that may want to harm him, then, he tested it. The cool water flowing around his hand and then roiling through his mouth was so refreshing. He detected no salt either.

After a couple more handfuls, he refilled his waterskin and began making a fire. He placed some rocks from the creek around the flames to hinder them from spreading and then laid on the ground. Leaves cushioned his back and his gear bag was under his head.

As the suns disappeared and Ash closed his eyes, the sounds of nature dwindled, allowing him to drift off. He wasn't sure if he was just becoming accustomed to the noise, or if all the creatures had suddenly decided to be silent for their own reasons.

Plans Come Together

Kane and Borg had ironed out the details to their plan so that everything was accounted for. Or so they hoped. They would wait for night when it was easier to creep about, sneak into the black tower, and steal the obelisk.

They assumed there would be guards inside the palace or Aros himself. If it was Aros, one of them would divert his attention elsewhere while the other tried to destroy the obelisk. If there was a guard, well, the guard would most likely be struck down. Kane didn't care that he may need to shed the blood of an enemy.

Once the obelisk is in their possession, Kane would call for a dragon and escape with Augustus. Kane only *hoped* that the dragons would hear and heed his call for help.

Borg entered Kane's hut unannounced, a grim look on his face.

"What is it?" Kane asked.

"You must come with me," he replied. "Hurry!"

Kane threw on his cloak and they stormed out, rushing across the encampment as quickly as possible.

"Move quietly," Borg whisper shouted.

Kane followed the goblin silently. Their footsteps as light as the touch of a feather. They scrambled through the camp until the tents and ramshackle huts disappeared and the landscape transformed into a vast plane of grass and rocks. Kane could see the lights from a city in the distance.

How normal humans could live so closely with a horde of monsters without noticing, Kane would never know.

Shortly ahead, there was a small group gathered. Borg motioned for Kane to stay low and he did. They crept up on the huddle, hiding behind a rock and peeking around its edges.

A couple of the members held torches which allowed enough light for Kane to see Aros. The demon king sat on the ground, cross-legged. His hands were in front of him and Kane could hear him muttering something but was unsure of what he was saying. Then, he realized it was a different language altogether.

After a moment, Aros stood, summoning a sphere of shadow into his palm. It had a faint, eerie glow about it. Almost like the dimmest light possible was in the sphere's center.

He raised it above his head and then slammed his palm into the ground. It shook.

The group scattered away from where Aros struck the ground. It was beginning to tear. A crack formed, no more than four feet in length and three feet wide. Aros began chanting again.

His foreign speech transformed back to English.

"Rise, my children!" he said excitedly. "Rise! Take your place next to me! Join me in this unholy endeavor!"

As if that weren't horrifying enough, whispers began issuing from the rift. Kane could feel his heart hammering in his chest.

A pair of dark, slender fingers slowly reached out from the pit. They gripped the ground, and whatever it was began pulling itself up. A creature emerged, its head coming out first. The thing had eyes like orange pits of fire.

All but Aros recoiled from it and the others that were joining them. Three of them in all. They stood around the same height as Aros. Probably around six feet tall. They all had a grayish skin tone nearing black. Each had blazing eyes and tall pointy ears.

Greasy, stringy hair hung down to their shoulders and the only clothes they wore looked like a loincloth. Their fingers and toes ended in claws, and they had canines like fangs when they spoke.

Kane couldn't understand anything they were saying. For the first time in a long time, Kane felt real fear strike through him. His hands and legs trembled, and if not for Borg, he would have been frozen in that spot forever.

Back in Augustus' prison, he relayed what Borg had just shown him.

"I remember Aros talking about them," he admitted. "His Princes of Darkness, he called them. They're demons like him. Although, he's clearly far worse, but they are still powerful creatures. They will be more ravenous and bloodthirsty than he, I think."

"What are we supposed to do about them?" Kane asked.

Augustus shook his head. "I wish I had all the answers, but I don't. I only have some. Perhaps, Gethin will know more."

"You may be right."

Kane's finger tapped lightly on his lip. "I say we move forward with the original plan. The obelisk *must* be destroyed.

If we can get it out of here, maybe we can figure out how to do that."

Augustus nodded. "Very well. When will you do it?"

"I'm not sure," Kane admitted. "After what I just witnessed, I'm curious how much more information I can find out before we leave. Everything we can learn before the war will be helpful. I don't want all this to have been for nothing."

"I understand. Although, I admit, I'm not fond of waiting here while you and the goblin lay siege to the tower. Three is stronger than two, after all."

"Yes, that's true, but we will be more inconspicuous just the two of us."

"But I can help," Augustus argued.

Kane considered it for a moment. A thought formed and he smiled wryly. "How do you feel about being a diversion?"

Augustus raised his eyebrows inquisitively. "Tell me more."

The Landes Forest

T he two girls were all packed up and ready to move out on their quest to find the Sword of Pescilon—the weapon that would be vital in the destruction of Aros. Quinn visited Gethin one evening to discern from her where they could possibly find such a weapon.

Quinn was surprised—but probably shouldn't have been—to find that Gethin had been expecting her. The Goddess, Queen of the Fae, or whatever title she was going by, had been rooted in deep thought to feel for the sword's location.

"The Landes Forest is where you will find the Bane of Darkness," Gethin had told her.

When Quinn met Kailani at the fountain in the center of town, she noticed that the Atlantean didn't look as sour as the last time they'd spoken. Quinn was happy she chose Kailani to accompany her on the mission.

"Ready?" Quinn asked.

"Yes. Did you find out where we will be going?"

"Landes Forest," Quinn answered. When Kailani waited for more details, she chuckled and said, "It's the largest forest in a place called Europe. Lady Gethin said she could feel it's power there, although, it was very faint. It's probably buried underground or in a cave, which would be funny considering it's the Bane of Darkness."

"Excellent," Kailani said. "Shall we?" She gestured towards the jungle. They would be travelling by water. It was the quickest way to travel besides flying by dragon back but they didn't want to take any of the dragons away for this. It was possible they wouldn't return in time for the coming battle.

The two girls clasped hands as they waded into the sloshing water of the sea. Kailani's abilities never failed to mesmerize Quinn. They propelled through the water at break-neck speeds. Landes Forest would be beneath their feet soon.

Once at the forest, Quinn used her magic to conjure all the water that had clung to them, leaving them dry and refreshed. Quinn was excited to start the journey. The sight of the forest in front of them, however, left her with a sense of impending doom. She began to fear that they would fail to find the sword in time.

Before them were lofty trees that stretched toward the sky, bushes and thickets, and a plethora of flowers. The plant life appeared to be infinite. She closed her eyes, breathing deeply, listening to the chirruping of the birds. Even as beautiful as Asmaria was, there were still many extravagant places on Earth.

"So, where do we start?" Kailani asked.

Quinn looked around. "Gethin said we would have to forge our own path and I'm beginning to think she meant that literally." There were several trails already made within the forest and Quinn highly doubted they would find what they were looking for if they only travelled where others had already been.

"Great," Kailani commented. "Let's get started, I guess."

So they did. They began trudging through the bushes, Kailani hacking away at the thicker of the brush with her chakram. The sun continued to fall as they plundered deeper into the forest. As dense as it had begun, Quinn was surprised to find that it could become denser.

"This is useless," Kailani complained as they walked into a small clearing. There were still trees, however, the smaller plants that made it difficult to walk through had vanished momentarily.

"Let's take a break."

They sat on the ground, backs leaned up against trees and sipped on water. "Regretting taking on this quest yet?" Quinn asked, breaking the silence.

The Atlantean seemed to consider it for a moment. "No. I wanted to do something, to be helpful in some way. I feel like…" she trailed off, looking at her twiddling fingers.

"What? You feel like what?"

She looked at Quinn. "I feel like I haven't done anything since we left Atlantis. I'm just kind of always *there*. I want to feel useful."

Quinn tilted her head at the girl. She hadn't been expecting that and she wasn't entirely sure what to say. "Well, I'm sorry you have felt that way. I'm sure we've all been there at some point. I know that we're all glad you came, especially Kane."

Kailani made a scoffing sound. "Yeah, that's why he ran off to join Aros, right?" She was looking up, blinking rapidly.

"That has nothing to do with you," Quinn said. "I don't claim to understand what he's thinking, but I will say this, I've never seen him as happy as when he's with you."

That seemed to do it. A low sob escaped Kailani's lips and a lonely tear streaked down her cheek. "Really?" she asked.

"Of course. I've known Kane my whole life and I can see that he's crazy about you."

"Then why'd he leave?" Her eyes were pleading for clarity.

"I don't know," she admitted. "However, I *do* trust him. You should too."

Kailani nodded. "Thanks."

"For what?"

"Bringing me along. Being so kind to me."

"Ready to kick this quest's butt?" Quinn asked with a smile.

The Atlantean smirked, rising to her feet and stretching out a hand. "Let's do it."

The first day in the Landes Forest flew by; time flies when you're struggling through the woods. They were unsuccessful in finding the sword on the first day, however, as the day turned to night, Quinn could see a faint trail of golden light along the ground. Kailani sounded unbelieving when Quinn mentioned what she was seeing. It was as if the magical sword were somehow calling out to them, guiding them to where it rested. Almost as if it wanted them to find it.

Falling

The appearance of the faint trail of golden dust made Kailani and Quinn realize they might need to search in the dark. They worried that it would vanish with the daylight so they laid down and got a few hours of rest before packing their things back up and continuing on.

Insects sang their nightly songs as they chopped and stomped their way into the dark forest. Quinn carried a torch, careful to not let it send the woods into a blaze.

"Where is this thing?" Kailani grumbled. "The sun will be up soon."

Quinn knew she was right. They would have to halt their progress if the trail disappeared, although at the moment, she would welcome some more rest. "It can't be much further. We've been searching for hours. This forest can't be *that* big, right?"

Then, just as the sun was beginning to peek over the horizon, they found something. It almost looked like the trail was disappearing, but then Quinn realized that there was a small cranny amongst a pile of rocks. It was a narrow slit and the trail continued into it. She might have missed it had they not been looking for something that could hide a magical weapon.

They ran to it, nearly tripping over their feet and the debris of the woods. "It's like a cave or something!" Kailani said excitedly. "Finally!"

"Do you think we should take a break before we go in?" Quinn asked.

Kailani nodded. "That's probably a good idea. There's no telling what sort of excitement awaits us in there."

And that's what they did. They made a small fire and ate some crackers, drank some water. The parts of sky that Quinn could see through the trees was a vibrant show of pink, orange, and dark blue.

They began sharing stories with each other of their childhood. Quinn found her cheeks hurting from smiling. She and Kailani hadn't yet developed a close friendship, but now she could almost feel one blossoming.

After taking a long break, the morning sun causing dew to gather on the leaves of trees, the two warriors began inspecting the crevice of a cave. It was so narrow that Quinn wasn't sure they'd be able to squeeze through. With some work though, they were able to just make it inside.

Quinn went first, sliding down into the dirty cranny. She fell a couple of feet, bumping her knees and elbows on rocks and tree roots. When she landed, she rolled and climbed to her feet. Her eyes darted around, examining the cave. Narrow rays of sunlight broke through cracks in the ceiling. It wasn't enough to see very well, but it was adequate enough to see that there was nothing else in the chamber, safe for dirt, rocks, and a tunnel leading deeper underground.

"It's safe to come in, but watch the rocks!" Quinn called out to her friend.

Kailani slid in shortly after, cursing as she landed the same way Quinn had. She got to her feet, brushing herself off and looking around. "How are we supposed to see anything?" she asked, squinting.

Quinn was wondering the same thing. "I have an idea," she said. She looked down at the golden trail that lead into the tunnel. Pulling a waterskin from her bag, she pulled the stopper and waved her hand, a small sphere of water forming in her palm. It hovered a couple of inches above her hand.

Kneeling down, Quinn passed the orb of liquid through the golden dust. When she stood back up, the ball of water had begun to glow softly. "How did you do that?"

She didn't know what had led her to try it. "I don't know, I just had a feeling that it would work."

"Well, we're fortunate that you were right."

"Let's find that sword," Quinn responded, determined to complete their quest as quickly as possible.

They started toward the tunnel, Quinn in the lead. She went through the entrance tentatively, careful to watch for sliding dirt and rock. Cobwebs and dangling roots littered the tunnel. It was clear that no one had been down there in ages. Every so often Quinn had to pull out her dagger to cut some of the debris away.

They had been marching down into the Earth for, well, she didn't know exactly how long it had been. Her back was aching and her breath was becoming steadily more labored.

"Will this ever end?" she asked.

Kailani was breathing just as hard. "I sure hope so."

As if they had spoken it into existence, the tunnel was finally levelling out and opening up. The tunnel ended and the two found themselves on a ledge. There was enough room for them to stand side-by-side, but not much more. As far as Quinn could tell, they were in a massive cavern with a high ceiling.

She lifted her hand, her fingers fluttering around in slow, calculated movements as the glowing sphere moved around the cavern effortlessly. There was a chasm beneath their feet and she couldn't seem to find the bottom. In front of them, protruding from the ledge, was two identical bridges of rock. The golden trail had vanished, leaving no trace of which path they should take.

Quinn recalled the light source. "Looks like we have a *very* important choice to make," she noted. "What do you suppose happens if we choose wrong?"

"Nothing good," Kailani replied. "Do we split up?"

"I don't know. I feel like we have to pick a path and hope it's the right one, although, if we guess wrong at first, the other can continue on."

"I don't like this," Kailani admitted, "but I'll go first."

"What? Are you crazy?" Quinn turned too quickly, her foot slipping on small rocks. She nearly lost her footing.

"Not at all. Gethin picked you for this quest for a reason. If one of us *has* to continue past this point, it's you."

Quinn admitted to herself that she had a point there, although, she didn't want to admit it. "Still, I can't do this without you. Gethin chose me for a reason, just as I chose you for a reason."

"Yes," Kailani said, nodding. "To make sure this is successful. This is how we do that."

Picking the left path, she began creeping forward and Quinn could see a slight shake to the girl's legs. Quinn could feel her own hands shaking as she watched her friend put one foot in front of the other. However, with each step, Quinn's angst seeped away. It looked like they had chosen correctly. The bridge was holding.

Then all her confidence was winked away. After reaching roughly halfway across the narrow bridge, the rock began to crumble. As if happening in slow motion, Quinn saw the rocky path begin to turn to rubble and Kailani was being swept into the abyss.

Princes of Darkness

A white plume rolled from Kane's mouth in the early morning's frigid air. He'd grown accustomed to the climate and it didn't bother him as much as when he'd first arrived. Borg was standing to his right, and everywhere else were the vile creatures the demon king had called from the squalor in which they hid.

There were beings referred to as ghouls, although, to Kane they were essentially just zombies. Aros had used some sort of necromancy magic on the corpses, bringing them back to, well, not life, but something like it. Their bodies were reanimated and pulled themselves from the eternal slumber beneath the dirt.

Kane thought to himself how out of all the beasts around him, the ghouls were the creepiest. They did nothing but stand there or wander around aimlessly and he couldn't see anything behind their eyes; some had no eyes at all, just empty sockets. They made no sound and felt no pain. Some of them had limbs or other various body parts missing and no one seemed to care. They were fodder.

The ghouls wouldn't be useful for much other than to get in the way, and Kane was relieved that they were bodies that had already passed on and not humans being possessed.

Along with ghouls, there were goblins, trolls, wraiths, giants, and a single banshee. Borg told Kane that this was the last banshee on Earth; all of its clanmates had died and, with her the banshee race would die out completely. The wraiths and banshee looked human enough. Their eyes is what set them apart. Wraith eyes were nearly the opposite of any human's wherein they were pits of white surround like black. The banshee looked like an old, withered lady except for the dark purple eyes in her head. Borg told Kane of the voice of the banshee; a scream from her was high enough to cripple the strongest of foes.

The giants would have looked rather human as well if not for their height and thickness. Each one had long hair, both male and female, and a face that looked disformed. They grunted a lot when spoken to and didn't seem to hold onto much intellect; however, Kane figured they would do a lot of damage in battle with the large clubs and hammers they toted around.

The trolls were probably some of the ugliest things he'd ever seen. Their skin was mostly a dark shade of green. Some of them had splotches of gray here and there, and most of them had plentiful warts.

They weren't small either but weren't quite as large as the giants. The trolls were closer to around seven feet, and where the giants were thick and muscular, the trolls were fat and jiggly. Kane didn't think they were smart enough to wield weapons. They were barely intelligent enough to strap on the loincloths covering their dirty business.

The goblins all looked very similar to Kane's new ally, Borg. Short and greenish with sharp teeth, claws and crimson eyes.

They wore boots and most of them carried daggers or small knives, others had short swords attached to their hips.

Even being next to all these creatures, smelling their stench of rotted flesh and meat, none of them frightened Kane as much as the demons standing behind Aros at the top of the stairs leading into the dark tower. Their faces were tilted down while their eyes peered up, making them appear all the more sinister.

They had been given cloaks similar to the one Kane wore and even in the brightness of day, their eyes blazed as they scanned the gathered troops.

"My beloved army," Aros began with a wicked smile. "I introduce to you, the Princes of Darkness. I have finally summoned them from the pits of the abyss to join me on Earth, their rightful place!"

He waved his arm at the creatures, beckoning them to step forward at the top of the steps. They did so, a reluctant look on their evil faces.

"Bal'lak, Delmith, and Glishem are my sons and you shall show them the respect they are due. My Princes of Darkness answer only to me. Is that understood?"

A resounding roar of agreement echoed from the gathered army of beasts. Kane felt his knees knocking together. He needed to get out of there; the longer he stayed in the midst of all the evil, the higher the chances of him being outed as a traitor.

The princes smiled menacingly and Kane had the feeling they would tear anyone in the dark lord's army apart if given the chance.

The crowd dispersed and Kane followed Borg back to his tent. Once inside, the goblin's hands went to his hips. He paced around, shaking his head. "This is bad, very bad," he said.

"Why is this so bad?"

"King Aros may be more evil than his sons," Borg continued, "but he at least has control over his temper. I have heard tell of times in the past, long ago, when the Princes of Darkness roamed the Earth more freely. They decimated entire groups of people who slighted them, killing for the pure enjoyment of it. They are truly terrifying."

"Aros is still the main goal," Kane replied. "Whether they're in the fight or not, we have to focus on defeating him. What happens to the princes if we kill Aros? Do you think they'll die as well?"

Borg's four-fingered hand went to his stubbly chin, rubbing in thought. "I wouldn't count on it. I fear we will have to deal with each one separately. They're bound to be weaker than the king, however, I wouldn't take them lightly."

"Agreed," Kane said, nodding his head. "Do you have any idea when Aros intends to attack Asmaria? Assuming that's his plan. I feel that he's keeping me in the dark with certain details."

"I'm afraid that information has not been passed along to me. The demon king does not require my counsel much these days."

"I'll need to learn as much as I can of what he's planning before we make our escape," Kane replied. "I guess there's never been a better time to practice my sneaking and eavesdropping."

"Be careful, whatever you do," Borg said, a look of concern on his face. "King Aros is no fool."

"Why, Borg, are you saying you care about my well-being?"

Kane smirked at his question.

Borg flushed. "What? No! I'm just saying—"

"Oh don't backtrack now, Borg," Kane interrupted. "You love me. Admit it."

Kane couldn't help but snicker when Borg waived his hands dismissively. "Oh, shove it, boy."

The night wasn't exactly the best concealment when the fiendish leader could command shadows but it was better than the day. Kane pulled his black cloak closely over his shoulders and creeped his way through the encampment of troops. They didn't pay him much mind anymore.

At first, a lot of the creatures attention was drawn to Kane any time he went outside of his little hut. Now, they keep their looks mostly to themselves as they've grown accustomed to his presence. He admitted to himself that it was rather odd, a human amongst monsters.

He crouched down around some small bushes near the tower. There was a giant sitting near the steps of the tower with a spiked club sitting across its lap. The white hair dangled in front of his eyes as he lifted a rock and hurled it passed the giant. It clattered a few feet away, drawing the giant's attention. The massive humanoid stood and stepped away, investigating the noise. Kane ran past him and up the steps with the tail of the cloak billowing behind him. He was inside the edifice and gently closed the door. It was dark but the oil lamps cast about feint light. The shadows danced across the floor.

Kane skittered through the main hall to the stairs like the last time he'd been in there. He went slow and steady, careful not to make any noise. There was no guard at the door to the stairs. After several minutes, he was back at the top just outside the door that leads to the throne room and houses the obelisk.

The door was already ajar. Kane inched closer, peering through the crack with one eye. Hushed conversation met his ears.

"…please, master, let me have some fun. You have a prisoner, no?"

It was like hearing a million insects crawling across the floor melded into voice. That was the best way Kane could describe it to himself. One of the princes was speaking to the demon king.

"There is a prisoner, yes," Aros replied, "but he is… off limits."

A snarl escaped one of the demons. "But, father, I *need* meat."

"In time, my child. I may yet have use for the man. Before it's all over, I will let you tear Augustus to shreds, but for now, you will cease this begging. Do you understand?"

"Yes, master," the three princes said in unison.

"Now then," Aros continued. "The eclipse approaches. Nigh is the time for our march upon the island. The three of you must be ready to carry out my orders. You shall lead the army to the enemy's shores. Blunder their homes and sink their island into the seas."

"Yes, master. We are ready," one of them said.

"Very good. I must venture out of our camp in three days. I won't be gone long."

"Where will you go?"

"That is none of your concern, Glishem," Aros lectured. "Your job is to ensure no one enters this tower. Understand?"

"Yes, master," they said in unison again.

Kane finally felt that he had enough information to take back to Asmaria. Aros would be taking a leave of absence;

a better opportunity would not arise. His hope was that the Guardians didn't hold his fake treason against him too harshly. Even more importantly, he hoped Ash would forgive him.

In the next three days he would need to plot out everything with Augustus and Borg. They needed to destroy the obelisk before escaping. The Princes of Darkness would be guarding the tower and if they raised the alarm, the entire army of creatures would be upon them instantly. Kane's mind was rolling through the plans he'd made so far as well as the information he'd just learned.

The final part of the plan would be to escape on the backs of the dragons. Kane could only wish that they would hear his call and answer in earnest.

Shal, the Protector

Quinn reacted so quickly that she surprised even herself. Thrusting her hand out, water erupted from her palm as if her body was made of it. The glowing orb was floating around haphazardly; Quinn's concentration was on saving her friend. Her body was straining.

The liquid rushed to catch Kailani, swooping down like the tentacle of an octopus. The water caught the girl, enveloping her body entirely. The weight of holding the water with another person inside was enough to nearly yank Quinn off the ledge as well. She yelled, no words, just a yell of desperation to pull the water and Kailani back up to the ledge.

Quinn pulled with all her might, and after several gut-wrenching seconds, succeeded. Kailani splashed onto the ledge where the two girls collapsed, both competing to see who could breathe harder.

"Th-thanks," Kailani managed to sputter out.

Through labored breaths, Quinn replied, "Don't... mention it." She urged the floating orb to return to her hand, both arms trembling. Conjuring elemental magic was taxing on the body enough without hauling a body from a deadly chasm. She worried that she would pass out from the energy her body had consumed especially considering how fatigued she already was from the days of travel and little sleep.

After they'd caught their breath, they sat up and eventually wrangled their feet back beneath themselves. Quinn could see Kailani's legs shaking; she seemed to not want to be anywhere near the edge of the abyss and Quinn didn't blame her.

She looked to the right path. "Well, I guess we know which way to go for sure now."

"Or," Kailani argued, "both paths are the same and whoever constructed this expects us to figure out another way across."

Quinn had to admit she had a point. "Okay, let me try something."

She took a steadying breath, closing her eyes. When she opened them, she pushed more water from the orbless palm, although this time, she conjured it to wash over the remaining rocky bridge. When the path was covered, Quinn squeezed her hand into a fist.

The Atlantean tattoo on her arm flared and the water solidified into ice. Kailani looked at it incredulously.

"Great," she said, "now we can skid off the ice to our deaths."

Quinn rolled her eyes. "Just come on. We should be fine now." And they were.

Quinn lead the way across, confident that her ice bridge would hold up even if the rock beneath didn't, although, neither gave away. Upon reaching the opposite, Quinn heard Kailani release a held breath. They were on another ledge that lead into another tunnel travelling deeper underground.

It was cold and became colder the further they ventured. Neither of them had dressed appropriately for the mission. Growing up on a tropical island did Quinn no favors in acclimating to the cold and, although Kailani lived her whole life under the earth, the magic in Atlantis never allowed its people to freeze.

They both shivered and Quinn wished she could free up her hand to rub away the gooseflesh that had pricked up on her arms.

"If we don't find this sword soon," Kailani began, "I may just lose my mind."

"I'll lose mine with you," Quinn half joked. Then, "I think the tunnel is widening up ahead." She squinted into the darkness and confirmed to herself that she was correct. The tunnel was becoming taller and wider, and then finally, it opened up into a decent-sized chamber.

There was a single sliver of light shining down from the ceiling and Quinn couldn't fathom how it was shining down considering how deep underground they were. They walked around the cavern, searching for anything that could lead them to the sword from there.

"Look at this," Kailani said.

When Quinn turned, the Atlantean was holding what looked like a small, jagged chunk of glass. Upon closer inspection, however, Quinn realized that it was rock or mineral of some kind. She began to wonder…

"May I?" Kailani handed it to her.

Quinn placed the mineral in the beam of light which multiplied the beams and casted them all around the chamber. Quinn could see a little better and found there to be more of the same rocks lying around, some embedded into the ground, walls, and ceiling.

"We just need to find the perfect spot and angle to place it and we should be able to see fairly well," Kailani observed.

"Right," Quinn agreed, looking around. There was a small

square stone on the ground just beneath the first beam of light. Quinn put it down and began turning it different ways until, finally, the room lit up with light. Quinn dropped her hand that was holding the orb. The light vanished and the water splashed the ground.

"Let's hope we don't need that to get out of here," Kailani said, a hint of annoyance in her voice.

"I'm sorry," Quinn replied. "My arm is just exhausted." Her arm shook and aches arced up and down.

"Look," Kailani pointed behind Quinn. The mage turned to find a large sword glittering into existence as if it were made of light. There was a cylindrical stone jutting up from the floor that held the sword captive.

"Wow," she marveled.

The sword had a double-edged blade and a golden handle with white crystals inlaid around the edge. Quinn found it to be utterly beautiful.

"Hello, dears," a cool voice drawled from somewhere in the room.

Both girls jumped and searched frantically for the source of the voice. Out of one corner of the cavern stepped a creature that was reminiscent of a human. It looked female with bright yellow hair cascading down over her shoulders and stopping just short of her navel.

Her irises were golden and bright. She glanced at them hungrily. The thing even wore a white dress, making her look innocent and pure, but the energy wafting from her was nothing but innocent. Quinn felt that this creature had taken a few lives.

The main characteristic that gave Quinn pause and told her this thing wasn't human, was the tail jutting out from the back of her dress and flicking along the floor. It looked like that of a scorpion.

"Who are you?" Kailani asked.

"I am Shal, protector of the Sword of Pescalon," she replied. "And you are?" She said those three words as if each was its own sentence, slowly.

"I'm Quinn and this is Kailani. We're here to—"

"I know why you're here," Shal interrupted. "You aim to steal the sword from me. You plan to use it for your own benefit, to destroy the world."

"No, that's not true," Quinn argued.

A look of confusion flashed across Shal's face and then vanished. "Then you are not here for the sword?"

"Well, no, we are," Quinn back tracked. "It's just that we don't want it for our own well-being. We need it to destroy Aros, the king of demons."

Shal laughed and laughed. "You expect me to believe that story? No, I think not. Run along now while I still allow you to leave with your innards. It has been terribly long since I've had visitors, and I will have fun slaughtering you two."

"Listen, lady," Kailani said with resolve, "we are not leaving without that sword."

"Very well," Shal replied with a smile.

The fabric beneath her dress began to writhe and then two more arms or legs popped out of the sides of her midsection. It was impossible to tell which because they weren't human like the rest of her. They were spindly like a scorpion, matching the tail that was now curled over her head, poised to strike.

Shal hissed as the girls prepared to fight. Kailani's chakram flew into her hand and she held it up defensively. Quinn's palms were facing toward Shal, water conjured in front of each.

"You get the sword, I'll handle this *witch*," Kailani told Quinn.

"What did you call me?" Shal shouted, her voice low and disturbing now. It made Quinn's skin crawl.

Shal didn't wait for a response; the creature lunged at Kailani, her tail stabbing at the girl with the tip of the stinger as if it were a venomous spear. Quinn watched Kailani block the first strike with her chakram before deciding to move her feet. She ran for the sword.

Reaching it, Quinn wrapped her small hands around the swords hilt and began heaving with everything she was worth. It wasn't budging in the slightest. She grunted with frustration and the effort, her muscles straining, the skin of her fingers screaming in pain.

She fell on her rear sending a wave of pain through her bones. "It's not coming out!" she shouted, glancing back at the fight.

Kailani dodged another tail strike and sliced at Shal, catching one of her scorpion legs. The creature howled in pain as dark green ichor poured from the wound.

"I'll kill you!" she screamed.

"Hurry!" Kailani yelled at Quinn.

She had to come up with something quickly. An idea suddenly clicked in her brain. Gethin had chosen Quinn for a specific reason. She knew something about this place that no one else did, yet she couldn't reveal too much, forever shrouded in mystery.

Quinn stood and let her palms hover just above the surface imprisoning the blade. She conjured the tiniest bits of water and sent them flowing into the minute cracks that existed within the rock.

A squeeze of her fist and the ice ability activates. Ice expands. Quinn closed her eyes, blocking out the sounds of the battle raging behind her to the best of her ability. She conjured more water to flow into the rock and repeated the steps.

With each motion of transforming her water to ice, Quinn could feel the rock cracking and crumbling.

Finally, after what she guess was a couple of minutes, the cylindrical rock busted and crumbled away from the sword. It fell promptly into her hands and she held it up. The magnificent blade glistened.

"Nooooo!" Shal cried at the top of her lungs.

Quinn spun as Shal charged her. The tip of the sword met her throat.

"But I am the protector," Shal whined and Quinn thought she had actually seen tears brimming. "You mustn't take it. What will become of me?"

"That isn't really any of my concern," Quinn answered honestly.

Shal must not have approved of that answer because the next thing she did was try to kill Quinn. Much quicker than the mage had expected, the venomous scorpion tail came out of nowhere. It was mere inches from piercing her face when Kailani's chakram came flying from the left and sliced through the tail.

The creature had no time to wail as Quinn lopped off her head with one clean swing of the Bane of Darkness. At the end of her life, Shal's body disintegrated and settled into the floor of the cavern.

Quinn looked over at her friend and found her bleeding from several small wounds. She sat on the ground, breathing hard from the exertion. Above and all around them, a low rumbling issued, becoming louder. Kailani scrambled to her feet as the ceiling began to shake and give way. The light from the crystals vanished as rubble began to fill the chamber.

Piercing the Darkness

Kane was walking around the camp as he had done nearly every day, seeing what he could glean from the routines of the beasts in the enemy base. Nothing new or out of the ordinary had come to him, that is until he spotted Aros on the front steps of the tower with his sons.

There was only two days left before the demon king had said he would be leaving the camp for something unknown to all but himself. Kane had brought the news back to Borg and then to Augustus. Then, he'd taken the dragon whistle and conjured the winds to carry him several kilometers away from the camp where he would blow into it ten times.

He waited for an hour and then, concerned that someone would notice his absence and report it, he conjured the winds to carry him back. The dragons hadn't shown. They were especially keen to the frequency of the whistle and he knew they would be able to dial in on the device's location. He only worried slightly that they would show up at the enemy camp when he least expected them.

Now, however, Aros had a look on his face that appeared to be worried or concerned. He couldn't hear what Aros was saying to the princes, but when he was finished waving his hands around, one of them vanished within the shadows. Kane sauntered over cooly, his hands in the sleeves of his cloak.

"Everything alright, Lord Aros?" he asked.

Aros seemed to consider whether he would tell him or not. Then said, "A powerful artifact that I had wished to remain hidden has just been recovered by a couple of your old friends."

Instead of asking which friends, he first asked, "What kind of artifact?"

Aros smirked. "Let's just say I'd rather it stay hidden for all eternity."

That sounded rather ominous to Kane. "Which of the Asmarian swine was it?"

"Not sure," Aros replied. "I sense two weak females. I've sent Bal'lak to deal with them and recover the sword. Their bones will rot in that forest."

Kane bowed shallowly and then turned away, trying not to alarm the king. He had a sense of foreboding coming over him and he hoped it wasn't who he thought it was. They would never see it coming.

The two girls dove for the tunnel, Quinn taking the lead. She found the sword to be giving off a brighter light than the glowing orb of water had provided. She ran, crouching as she went up the slope of the tunnel grasping Kailani's hand the entire time. Quinn refused to lose her on this quest.

She could feel the Atlantean's ragged breath on the nape of her neck. "Don't stop!" she shouted, anything to encourage her to keep her feet moving. The tunnel was collapsing behind them; Quinn could hear it, like a thunderstorm inside her ears.

Holding the sword out in front of her body was becoming exhausting. She told herself to keep going, to not give up and it would all be over soon. They escaped from the lower tunnel and ran across the rocky bridge. The ice had long melted and Quinn didn't have ample time to create a new one with the earth trying to drop on their heads.

They made it into the upper tunnel and were both panting. Quinn was all but dragging Kailani along. Finally, they made it into the initial chamber where the entrance was. They fell into the space in a heap. It seemed like the collapsing stopped with the previous tunnel.

For an eternity, all that existed was the haggard breathing that filled the chamber and the liquid fire that swirled in Quinn's lungs. That fire spread evenly throughout her limbs. She shook with fatigue. Afte awhile, Quinn looked at her friend who was breathing just as hard and shaking as well.

"We did it," Quinn was able to muster.

"That we did," Kailani replied.

They didn't dare attempt to move from that spot for a long time. When they finally decided to sit up, the daylight shining through the crevice was dimming. "We better get a fire going before the darkness settles in," Kailani noted.

She climbed out of the cave and then Quinn followed after, handing the sword to her. Looking at it again as she did gave her a sense of great accomplishment.

They made a fire directly outside the cave, neither of them feeling up to traveling.

"My, what have we here?" A voice asked from the shadows. Again, the two girls jumped and Quinn wondered what was going on that the universe would send two creepy creatures to seemingly melt from the shadows to attack them.

"Ugh, what now?" Kailani asked, exasperated. "Have we not endured enough?" She shouted the question into the sky.

Several meters away, a shadow morphed and a humanoid shape formed. The thing had blazing red eyes, long stringy hair, and a skin complexion that made Quinn feel ill. Its fingers were long and the nails were more like claws.

"Who are you?" Quinn asked.

He bowed low as he said, "I am Bal'lak, Prince of Darkness, son of King Aros."

"Prince of Darkness?" Kailani asked. "Sounds lame."

Bal'lak growled, "Lame? For that, you shall die slowly. I'll kill the other one quickly and then peel your flesh from your bones."

A stygian dagger manifested in both of the creature's hands and his smile grew from ear to ear. He charged the girls before they could get to their feet. Kailani had recovered only a bit of her strength and couldn't raise the Sword of Pescalon fast enough. As it swung in front of her, Bal'lak swatter it away with both daggers and simultaneously delivered a kick to her sternum.

The sword dropped to the forest floor as Quinn jumped into action, hurling water at him. Liquid swirled around both arms and she froze it. Bal'lak screeched with rage and pain before vanishing in whisps of shadow. He materialized standing over Kailani and was already bringing his onyx blades down.

Quinn flung blades of water at him, solidifying them as they soared through the air. They lacerated his chest and rocked him backwards enough to send his strike amiss. Kailani was able to kick his leg, tripping him, and scramble back to her feet. The beast snarled and dashed at Kailani.

The water mage's next attack missed. The water whip she'd conjured and flashed at him flicked behind him, missing by an inch. Quinn's heart got stuck in her throat. She was suddenly powerless to save her friend.

Much to Quinn's surprise, Kailani had moved quicker. All in one fluid motion, the Atlantean had thrown her chakram at Bal'lak, connecting with his upper thigh. It slowed him down slightly. As the circular blade left the girl's hand, she dived onto the sword, rolled and twisted back around facing the creature.

She raised the sword with no time left to spare and Bal'lak landed on it with his daggers raised overhead. They vanished as the red of his eyes dissipated and he crumbled into dust.

A roar of anguish, rage, ripped through the camp as Kane was relaying what had happened with Aros and Bal'lak to his goblin friend. Borg smiled as the sound echoed around.

"Sounds like your friends stopped the prince after all," Borg said.

The relief Kane felt was insurmountable, or so he thought. His relief was short lived as, for the second night in a row, no dragon showed up to his call for help. What would they do if the dragons ignored them?

Beauty is Deadly

Ash had made it out of the dense forest; at first, he'd thought the titanic trees were all there was, but then he found himself entering a ravishing meadow. It seemed to be a wheat field, although, he wasn't sure that's exactly what it was. Everything else in this realm had been somewhat different from Earth, why expect anything normal now?

In the three days it took to escape the forest, he'd climbed up one of their massive trunks a second time to get his bearings. It didn't leave him as exhausted as it had the first time. Perhaps his pacing was better the second time around.

Nothing had tried to kill him again, not yet, anyway. In between Ash and the palace was the meadow and a field of flowers that stretched for miles. Just past that laid another forest, however, this one looked less gargantuan. Ash could see the palace erected amongst the trees.

He was close enough—and the encroaching forest shallow enough—that he figured he'd reach its base by nightfall if he continued at the same quick pace he'd adopted upon entering the meadow. The three-foot-tall stalks of wheat-like vegetation began to ebb away, turning to flowers. Beautiful round petals of nearly every color, of course, the purple ones drew Ash's eye more than any.

There were insects mulling about the field of flowers. He expected them to be bees but he didn't recognize any of the little fliers. They were probably pollinators all the same, though.

About halfway through the field with a few hours of daylight left—he'd learned to anticipate the timing of the double suns of Tuvetal—Ash took a break, sitting amongst the flowers. He would learn how big of a mistake that was.

The young mage began flattening out some of the blooming flowers to lay down with his gear bag as a pillow. He closed his eyes for a moment before reopening them and pulling one of the flowers from the ground. He gave it a whiff, breathing deeply. The aroma assaulted his nostrils instantly.

It was more than just smelling good or sweet. The scent became his favorite—the peaches that were native to Asmaria. He hadn't known he could love a smell so much before being introduced to the juicy fruit. It reminded him of Quinn, the girl who'd shown him where the peaches grew wild in plenty. Ash smiled, sucking in more of the scent of the flower through his nose.

Suddenly, the sky went dark. It was as if the suns were controlled by a light switch that someone had flicked off. Laughter filled his head, dark and dastardly. He would recognize it anywhere. Ash jumped to his feet, the ground beneath him felt different, no longer a field of flowers. It writhed under him which made it difficult to keep his balance. Like he was surfing on a wave of worms.

What is happening? he thought.

Ash snapped his hands out to his sides, trying to conjuring

his lightning magic. Nothing happened. He took a deep breath, the laughing in his mind a crescendo, and tried again. Still nothing.

Panic attacked him. Ash's heart pounded and he could hear it ramming against his ribs. He was breathing haggardly. A shape moved in front of him and he felt a foot plant on his chest. He was sent sprawling onto the crawling ground. Orange flame ignited around him in a ring of fire as a masked figure pointed and laughed at him.

His father.

Augustus pulled the mask off to reveal a pale, bearded face. His teeth were yellow and gums black as he continued laughing. Ash stole a glance at the ground and found himself swimming in worms. Bile surged up from his stomach and caught in his throat.

"What do you want from me?" he roared at his father.

The man jumped into a crouch directly in Ash's face. "I want your life," the man growled.

Ash moved to punch him, but when his swing would have connected, Augustus disappeared. The world shifted, turning him upside down and suddenly, he was back on Asmaria. Aros sat on a throne in the middle of town, jutting up where the statue of Gabriel was supposed to be. The throne was made from blood and bone. His cronies led shackled Asmarians around the streets.

Anger flared inside Ash again and he tried to summon his magic once more. It was futile.

Wake up, Ash, a voice thundered in his head. He thought it was Raimir, but couldn't be certain.

"What?" he shouted. "Wake up from what?"

Am I asleep or something?

That made more sense than anything else. "Come on, Ash, wake up. Come on!" he yelled at himself, but nothing happened. An idea struck him.

In dreams, he'd always jerked awake when he felt the sensation of falling. If he could induce that, maybe he would wake up. Or, maybe it would kill him and all of this would cease to be his problem. He wasn't sure he cared.

Ash found his way up one of the buildings in the street, clamored over to the edge, and wasted no more time. He turned his back to the street and fell, as if doing a trust fall.

With a loud gasp, his eyes snapped open and Ash was blinded by the two suns even though they were nearly upon the horizon. How long had he been entranced? He jumped to his feet, his heart still beating rather quickly, and gathered himself. He took off at a jog, a feeble attempt at making up for the hours he'd just lost by the mind-altering flowers. If nothing else, he wanted to get out of that field as quickly as possible.

Penny

Ash made it out of the field and into the next forest by the end of the day. He hadn't made it to the palace thanks to being put into a nightmare state by the flowers. Ash had the sense that he was being watched again, and ever since the nightmare in the field his legs hadn't stopped shaking.

A fire crackled, brought to life by Ash's lightning; he found himself beyond relieved for the magic to be working in the waking world.

Looking around, Ash noticed why he had the feeling of being watched. It's because he was. There was a pair of round yellow eyes looking at him from a distance. Ash stared back, daring not to break the gaze in fear that if he looked away, the thing—whatever it was—would find a way to sneak up on him.

After a minute, the eyes winked out of existence. Ash's fear increased slightly, and then an owl landed next to him. He started, magic flaring to life in one palm. The owl studied him from the large rock it was perched on.

"Put that away before someone gets hurt," the owl screeched out. Ash didn't know why he was surprised to learn it could talk. Maybe it was because this one was normal-sized whereas everything else had been colossal, or maybe it was because the bird's beak moved rather than speaking to him telepathically like all the other creatures.

Ash found that his fear had seemed to melt away and he killed the arcing lightning. "So, you can speak," Ash said.

"Of course I can speak!"

Ash thought he'd offended the owl, if offending an animal was even possible.

"Sorry, it just took me by surprise."

The owl's head spun 360 degrees. "I don't see how. After meeting Raimir, nothing should come as a shock to *you.*"

Angrily, "You know Raimir? Where is he?"

The owl must have been able to sense the fury coming from Ash. It said, "Simmer down, young chap. The great galoot is a distant cousin of mine. This is all for your own good."

"How in the world is dumping me in a foreign jungle where everything that flies, slithers, or crawls wants me dead, for my own good?" he asked.

"It's all to make you stronger and to prove your worth," the owl replied.

"Prove my worth to who?"

"The king, of course," the owl said, shaking its head. "Raimir did his best to convince King Dolgotha to grant you passage into Tuvetal."

So the snake wasn't kidding about a king, Ash thought. He'd originally thought it unlikely that there was a ruler of that world.

The owl continued, "The king has *never* granted a human passage in all his immortal life. If humans were able to find a way to access Tuvetal, they would plunder it for resources.

Well, they'd try to, anyway."

"So, do all of you know everything there is to know about humans?" Ash asked, finding it spot on thinking that humans would come here to wreak havoc if given the means.

"Not all," the owl answered. "Most of us are rather intelligent, but some, not so much."

"Tell me this." Ash crossed his arms. "Why did Raimir ditch me? Why offer me no help whatsoever?"

"Leaving you to navigate your way to the palace is the king's doing. This is his test for you, not Raimir's. As far as giving you no aid, who do you think woke you from the maddening slumber of the stupefy flower? Who do you think sent me to tell you this? Do not blame Raimir for any of this. Be grateful for his friendship and guidance. The General is a wise and kind being, and you are fortunate to be under his tutelage."

All of these things Ash had never considered. His anger trickled away and his heart felt a bit lighter to know that he hadn't been abandoned by his friend's volition. "Raimir's a General?" was the question he asked next.

"Indeed," the owl answered.

The two of them spoke for a long time, trading stories from their respective worlds. Ash learned the owl's name to be Penny. He wasn't sure if she was a male or female before learning her name; Penny's voice was in an odd, in-between octave.

She wasn't magical in any way besides being able to speak and Ash learned that she could speak every language known, even those that belonged to different worlds outside of his Earth. Apparently, there are an infinite number of realms that exist—as far as anyone knows—and Penny need only lay eyes on a creature to know its language. He found that to be a rather useful ability.

Penny stayed with him through the night and it was the best sleep he'd had in a long time.

The following morning, Ash awoke to find Penny had gone. A message was scrawled in the dirt next to the smoldering remains of the fire.

Good luck.

Ash sent a mental "thank you" to Raimir before marching further into the woods. A couple of times, Ash startled some various life forms, causing the both of them to jump, however, none of them attacked. He also didn't see anything that was oversized.

Sometime around what he would call noon, the forest abruptly ended and the ground in front took a wild turn. The first piece of ugly landscape he'd seen thus far laid before him. It was a barren desert, safe for the creeping plants strewn about. There were several viny plants scattered throughout the weeds, and beyond that, the palace.

"Finally," he said to himself, releasing a breath and the stress of wondering if he was ever going to make it.

The vine plants had thick stalks that stood at least eight feet tall. There were more than he originally noticed and navigating through them was tedious work. He supposed he could just incinerate them with lightning, but that felt unnecessary. Ash continued to wind his way through the brambles.

Upon closer inspection, Ash could see dark red thorns covering most of the vines. Ash focused on the palace through the gaps in the greenery.

It reminded him more like the Aztec pyramids he saw on

the discovery channel once; constructed of a tan stone, the palace had steps that led up to the top, getting more narrow. He couldn't make out many details of the top of the pyramid-esque palace, it was too tall. Ash could already feel the dread seep into his already tired and worn muscles at the prospect of having to climb those steep steps.

A rustling sound stole his attention from the palace. Looking around, Ash didn't see anything moving at first. Then, he realized it was the vines. The closer ones were curling in towards him. He picked up his pace, but as he went, each vine within ten feet would stretch his direction.

The plants didn't implant fear into him like the nightmare fuel provided by the stupefy flowers, they just simply gave him the creeps. He could feel a chill run along his spine as he jogged through the thickets.

His luck was looking up as the vines were coming to an end. He could see the steps more clearly. That luck didn't last, however, because just before he reached the end of the creeping plants, the vines began to move much faster.

They all but launched at him, a dozen vines at least, although he wasn't counting. Each one wrapped around whatever they could grab onto despite his thrashing. The pain from the thorns was instant and the more the vines squeezed and crawled around his body, the more intense the pain became.

"Agh!" he screamed, conjuring lightning into his hands.

The plants were smarter than he could have suspected though; as soon as the purple arcs materialized, they were vanquished by the thorny vines as they wrapped around his hands, closing them into tight fists. The plants were only minorly singed along the surface.

Fine, Ash thought.

Unsure of where it came from, lightning struck in his brain in the form of an idea. Closing his eyes, Ash felt the deep well of magic within him and began pulling at it, collecting it in the center of his chest. Mustering all the strength his muscles would allow, he began to pull his arms him. He probably looked like a bodybuilder striking a pose.

When it felt right, the mage released all the pent up energy amassed in his center. With a guttural cry, his flexed arms thrust out and an explosion of amethyst left his body, blasting the plants away.

The murderous greenery was burned away and what was left turned to black ash. Ash coughed as the smoke filled his lungs. He shuffled forward, a great deal of exertion coming upon him.

The steps. He just wanted to make it to the steps of the palace. He was so close.

Ten feet.

Five feet.

Ash collapsed on the first step, peering at the clouds passing through the sky. He looked down, examining his arms, his entire body aching and throbbing. There were small holes and large, red welts where the thorns had pricked him.

Of course they were poisonous.

He didn't know if he had successfully proven himself worthy to the king of Tuvetal, but he had proven it to himself. He'd survived the retched place. Almost. Ash could feel his consciousness waning. Giving in to the pain and fatigue, Ash began to close his eyes. A large gust of wind and black enveloped him as he slipped into darkness once again.

To Steal an Obelisk

emon King Aros had been rather irritable for the past couple of days since Bal'lak left and presumably perished at the hands of the Asmarians he was sent to kill. More than once Aros had tossed one of his loyal vermin from the dark tower, smiting them in front of everyone as a warning to not mess with him. One of the unlucky giants found himself headless after doing something—Kane didn't know what—that the dark lord did not find favorable.

Kane and Borg had crouched behind a tent near the spire, watching Aros as he stalked away from the camp. They watched until he'd become a dot in their vision, even Borg whose vision was far greater than Kane's, confirmed King Aros had left. Their time to act was upon them with or without the dragons, although it was looking like it would be without. Still, Kane pulled the whistle free and blew into it for a few long minutes. The frequency was like that of a dog whistle—too high for the ears of any human.

To Kane's surprise, however, he saw many of the monsters in his midst turn their heads frantically in search of the high-pitched whistling. He and Borg made themselves look less suspicious, pretending to tie the laces of their boots.

The remaining two Princes of Darkness sat on the steps of the black-stoned tower, their evil eyes scanning left and right. They seemed to be taking their new post seriously. Kane was nervous and butterflies fluttered inside his stomach, but not in the good way, like when he and Kailani would hold hands.

He thought of her then. The white markings that ran along her arms, her hair that always seemed to be in a tight braid and smelled of sea salt. He yearned to see her again and hoped he lived long enough to do so.

Kane and Borg had freed Augustus from the pit, draping a hooded cloak over him to conceal his face. He moved with a hunch, keeping his face downcast so that no one could recognize him. He waited at the furthest point away from the tower while still remaining inside the perimeter of the camp. Now, they would wait for Augustus to commence the diversion.

They hadn't waited for long when columns of bright flame erupted from a couple of kilometers away. Shouts echoed all around the camp; Kane saw many of the members of the dark army running in the direction of Augustus. The explosive flames were moving, Augustus was running, leading them away. They abruptly stopped and Kane found himself surprised at the concern he felt for the man's well-being.

Kane glanced back to the princes; they remained at the base of the tower, however, they'd risen to their feet. "It's now or never. I don't think they're going to leave that spot," Kane told the goblin.

"Agreed," Borg said.

The little goblin sauntered forward first as the two had planned. "My Princes!" he called to them. "The sorcerer has escaped his prison! We must deal with him before he depletes the king's forces!"

Kane saw the two demons share some words but was unable to hear them, and then, Delmith followed Borg away and into the thick of the tents and huts. That just left Glishem for Kane to deal with. For now, he still had the element of surprise.

Without a second thought, Kane burst away from his hiding place. Not wanting to give the demon a chance to react, Kane hurled a massive wind at him. The prince was lifted off his feet and sent spiraling away with a loud cry of surprise. Kane didn't stop; he shouldered the door open and pull his karambits free. As he'd suspected, there were a couple of trolls in the main chamber of the tower. They looked up at him lazily. Kane dispatched them before they could move further.

As he ran up the spiral stairs, he wiped the dark goo that soiled his blades. The door to the throne chamber was locked. Kane collected a ball of wind in his palm and thrust it into the thick wooden door. It splintered immediately.

The room was empty, save for the flickering oil lamps, the throne, and the obelisk. Kane was breathing hard, but knowing his work wasn't finished, he knocked the throne over contemptuously with a swat of wind magic.

Once we destroy this, Aros will be one step closer to death, he thought.

Kane summoned a wind to wrap around the obelisk; dust flew around the room, blinding him. He squinted through the particles, trying to lift the obelisk from the floor. It was unnaturally heavy.

The wicked object wobbled, but something interrupted Kane. The sound of the door behind him banging open alerted him. He spun, spheres of white wind already swirling in his palms.

He steadied himself; it was just Borg. The goblin looked hopeful.

"Well?" he asked.

Kane shook his head. "It's incredibly heavy; I don't know how we're going to carry it out of here. I can bust through the rocks of the tower, but I don't know if I can keep them from burying us."

"Well, you better figure it out quickly. The princes will be back here any moment."

As if on command, the two demons materialized from the shadows on either side of the obelisk. Wicked grins adorned their faces.

"You thought it would be so easy?" Glishem whispered creepily, his voice raising the hairs along Kane's arms.

"Come on," Kane began, putting as much false confidence in his voice as possible. "Do you think this isn't all part of the plan?"

The sons glanced at one another suspiciously.

Suddenly, Borg yelled, "Now!" and sprang forth to fight.

He had a dagger in his hand, the demons wielding one in each of theirs. Kane joined next to the goblin with karambits flared. Shadowy blades clashed on steel. None of them were making any progress.

A voice interrupted the battle, "Enough!"

Kane's skin crawled. It was Aros. The demon king had melted from the shadows in a corner of the room. He and Borg began to backpedal toward the entrance. A wall of shadow filled the doorway, blocking their path. They were trapped. Kane had never felt so sure that he would die, not even when they'd fallen miles beneath the earth to Atlantis.

"You *really* thought you could steal my obelisk?" Aros asked, one corner of his mouth twitching upward. "You thought I didn't know of your plans all along?"

Kane was nonplussed. "What? How?"

Aros bellowed a wicked laugh. "You live in my camp, boy. I hear and see nearly everything."

That one word. 'Nearly'.

Kane smiled. "Nearly everything? Then, I don't supposed you know our entire plan, do you?"

Aros crossed his arms and cleared his throat. "Enter," he commanded. The wall of shadow at the door dropped and someone was shoved in.

Kane stared at Augustus, once again bruised and beaten. Bloody saliva ran down his lips and into his beard. He had a cut above one eye and breathed harshly. "What happened?" Kane asked.

Augustus only shook his head.

"Now, how do you plan to escape then? That part I am not privy to, although, I don't think it matters much at this point. You've been captured and your plan has unraveled. There is no escape for you."

"That's where you're wrong!" Augustus shouted suddenly, his hands springing to life. Flame erupted, and it was so bright, that Kane had to shield his eyes. When it vanished, Aros laughed, waving away the shadows that nullified the fire magic.

"That was your escape plan?" he shouted with laughter. The princes soon joined in. Aros ceased laughing abruptly, a hand shooting towards Kane. A tendril of pitch black leapt at him and curled around his throat. The absence of air was immediate.

Aros slammed the boy into the wall of the tower over and

over. He felt as if the back of his head was caving in. He pulled his hands up, trying with all he had to conjure magic. More tendrils popped from the ground and wrapped around his wrists. His body was going to break.

It ended as quickly as it had begun. Kane vaguely saw movement from the side. A blade of flame lashed out from Augustus' hand and severed the tendrils holding onto him. He didn't see what caused it, but the wall behind Kane gave way, and he began tumbling into the open air. Kane felt a tugging sensation and his momentum slowing before losing consciousness.

Return of the Warriors

Quinn and Kailani were met with clapping and congratulatory cheers from the Asmarians flooding the streets near the Capitol building. It would seem Lady Gethin could either sense the girls or the Sword of Pescalon drawing near and alerted the Guardians. The other Asmarians followed the commotion and, slowly, a crowd had formed to wait for them.

They both smiled gleefully as they presented the Bane of Darkness to Gethin together. She took it with eyes full of pride. "I'm so proud of you two!" she beamed.

When Gethin took the blade, a weight was lifted from Quinn's entire body. She was flooded with relief and the fatigue of it all came crashing down. She wobbled, Kailani steadied her.

"Sorry," Quinn apologized. "I think I need to rest."

"Yes," Gethin called out loudly, "let us allow our heroes to have a brief respite before hearing their tale! I'm sure it's a good one and I *do* love a good story." She smiled at them softly and then they left the crowd behind.

"Want to crash at my house? It's closer than Atlantis."

"I would love to," Kailani accepted the invite.

Quinn had offered Kailani her bed and resigned to the couch, falling asleep faster than she thought possible. When she awoke, Kailani was waiting for her at the kitchen table. Quinn's mother baked some fresh bread and Kailani was eating it delightedly with drizzled honey.

Quinn rubbed the sleep from her eyes and moved sluggishly to join her friend. Her mother gave her a hug before the girl sat and began fixing some honey-drizzled bread for herself. Then she thought of Ash, wondering if he was okay and how his training was going. She had a feeling that if he had died, she would know somehow. Gethin probably would know too.

"How long did we sleep?" Quinn asked her mother.

The woman was wiping down the counters and replied, "It's been about thirty-five hours, I'd say."

"What? Thirty-five hours?" she echoed. "How has it been that long already?"

"Time flies when you're passed out and exhausted," Kailani answered. "Ready to go face the masses again?"

"Just about," Quinn said, shaking some leftover grogginess from her head. "Let me wake up a bit more and we can go."

The light in the sky was nearly gone when they made it to the Capitol. Gethin and the Guardians sat around the Sword of Pescalon, which was resting on a wooden table on the main floor. Quinn figured none of them wanted to let it out of their sight. They stood when they noticed the two young ladies approaching.

Leena pulled them both into a tight hug at the same time. "Not that I don't have faith in you two, but I was very worried. You never know what kind of danger you'll face out there."

Quinn began laughing and Kailani soon followed. "What? What's so funny?" Leena asked.

"I think you'll understand if we tell you everything that we just went through," Quinn replied.

They recounted the entire journey together, not leaving out a single detail. Gethin was the only one with an unreadable expression. The Guardians, however, became more wide-eyed and slack jawed as the story progressed.

When they told of Bal'lak, the son of Aros who'd been sent to kill them, Gethin's eyes showed fear. "It is fortunate that you found the sword," she told them. "I fear, without it, you would have perished. The sons of Aros are a wicked bunch."

"Sons," Avani uttered. "You mean there are more of them?"

She nodded. "Three in total if I remember correctly. They're not as powerful as the demon king, but what they lack in strength, they make up for in their lack of control."

A collective shudder went through them.

"So, what's next?" Kailani asked.

The Guardians appeared to not know as none of them answered. It seemed they were waiting for Gethin to respond. Gethin considered the question.

"There are travelers on their way here," she said. "We shall wait for them, and when they arrive, we will see what they have to say for themselves."

The Guardians looked as confounded as Quinn felt then. Dihren asked, "Travelers? Who could you possibly mean, My Lady?"

She waved her hand. "Oh, stop with the formalities already, all of you. Gethin is perfectly fine." Dihren looked abashed but quickly recovered. She closed her eyes and continued, "I sense four creatures quickly approaching, flying over the sea. Two of them are not human in any sense of the word. The other two, a white-haired young man and another who is older. I can't see much from him for he's shrouded in shadow."

Quinn's heart did a flip and, based on Kailani standing abruptly, she assumed she was thinking the same thing. Bora looked angry as she slammed a fist on the wooden table. "That has to be Kane, the white-haired boy. I'm going to ring his neck."

"I do not think it wise to act so rashly, child," Gethin said. Bora's anger appeared to ease at that. Maybe it was the matronly figure calling her 'child'. "I have a feeling they too will have quite the tale to tell. Whether they come with good tidings or bad, we shall listen to what they have to say. My guess is they will arrive by dawn."

Kane was awoken by the four-fingered slaps of his goblin friend. "Wake up, boy," Borg yelled over the wind.

Kane tried to sit up but was unable to without the assistance of Borg and Augustus who was sitting behind him. The familiar beat of wings filled his ears. He smiled as his head pounded.

"Vesta, you came," he said gratefully. He would have cried if not for the fear of the wind freezing his tears. The sun was almost up, the dimmest of light indicating that it would break the horizon in mere minutes. The island was close enough for him to make out its shape.

He was elated to be so close to home, yet he was worried about what would happen to them. Kane felt he would most certainly be imprisoned. Borg would probably be right there with him, or maybe exiled. Augustus, however, might be executed for all the pain and death he has brought upon the Asmarians. When Kane looked back at the man, he looked like he was thinking the same thing. His face was wrought with dread.

Borg, being a goblin, was nearly impossible to read. His face didn't always contort based on emotion like a person's.

Kane's entire body throbbed and ached and he was just ready to be on the ground. He'd felt a large knot and minor laceration on the back of his head. *Take me to the hospital, please,* he thought. Some heala would work wonders for his wounds.

"What happened?" he croaked, just then realizing his mouth was cotton dry. "I mean, how did we escape?"

Augustus answered, "Well, I was captured pretty quickly. Turns out, that banshee has a wicked voice. She screamed in such a high pitch that it knocked me off my feet and I had to cover my ears to keep my head from popping. Of course, they beat me bloody after that and dragged me to the tower. I figured it would benefit all of us if I didn't fight back until we were together."

Borg interjected, "And after I lured Delmith away from the tower, I waited until he was distracted enough and bolted. Aros knew our plans somehow, which you already know that. We had to leave the obelisk behind obviously, but seeing as we barely made it out alive, I consider ourselves lucky."

"Remind me how we made it out," Kane said, rubbing his head.

Augustus jumped back in. "When Aros was focused on you, your little friend here distracted one of the sons again."

"Then," Borg said with a scoff at the 'little friend' comment, "I rammed the wall with my shoulder. I had assumed you were okay enough to use that wind magic of yours to cushion our fall. Boy, was I wrong."

"You and Borg fell from the tower and I knew I didn't want

to wait around with all those demons, so I jumped. The dragon swooped in right under me and caught the two of you with its claws."

"It was pure luck that the great beast showed up at the perfect moment," Borg said.

A shiver went up and down Kane's spine. "Whew. Vesta, before I forget, I love you. You're awesome. Thanks for coming."

Something like a chortle came from the dragon as they floated down onto the training field. That was the only area on the island big enough for her to land without damaging buildings or something besides the mountains with the caves in which she dwelled, of course.

The sun was only just up and people already waited for them. Kane looked through the faces. He saw the Guardians, all with somber looks and crossed arms. Next to them stood someone that he found familiar, but wasn't sure who she was. He spotted Quinn with a smile on her face which brought one to his as well, despite feeling like his entire body was broken. Then he saw the girl who loved above all else—Kailani. His heart leapt with joy at the sight of her and it was almost enough to assuage the physical pain he felt. There was a small sad smile on her face. He knew he had a lot of explaining to do. One face he didn't find, no matter how hard he searched, was Ash's.

Scrutinized

As soon as Vesta's strong feet touched down on the training field, they were all surrounded by mages. The Guardians remained in front of the dragon's head with the auburn-haired woman beside them. The mage leaders had stern looks and the other woman looked slightly bemused.

With the help of Borg and Augustus, Kane slid unathletically off the back of the dragon. They held him up with his arms on their shoulders. Beneath one arm, Kane could feel August begin to shake intermittently. Vesta launched back into the air, sending Kane's white hair whipping across his vision, and flew back towards Frost Mountain.

"So, what do you have to say for yourself?" Bora asked quizzically. Kane could feel Augustus shrink behind him.

"Where do I start?" Kane asked.

"Start with why," Kailani blurted before anyone else could respond.

"Wait," Avani called out, his eyes narrowed and then flared wide as realization dawned on him.

With the long, matted hair, dirty beard and abused face, Augustus' identity had remained momentarily hidden. Avani's green eyes bulged and his hands whipped out in intricate patterns. The ground beneath Kane's feet shifted. He and Borg were flung aside by rolling terrain. After landing hard on his back, air leaving his lungs, Kane rolled to the side and wheezed. Kailani and Quinn were both at his side. He looked at Borg between pain-racked breaths and saw him being kept at the ground with flame-encased hands inches from his dark green face.

Kane looked at Augustus; Avani had him twisted into the ground and shackles of stone clamped around his hands. He looked terrified. Avani edged closer with his teeth grinding together. He looked furious. Kane could see that the stone was squeezing tighter on the man's hands as he began to groan and grimace.

The girls helped him to his feet and Kane felt the urge to protect Augustus. It was dumb and confusing. But they'd been through a lot together and he considered him a helpful ally, if not a friend.

It took a lot of strength and energy to lift his arms and conjure the wind magic, but when it came, he released it like a shove. Avani's feet swept out from under him and he fell. The stone vices crumbled back to the ground. Everyone turned to look at Kane as if he'd just committed a crime and, maybe he had. Kane could do nothing more than stand there, hanging onto the two girls weakly, and breathe raggedly.

The prison they were tossed into had been upgraded since the last time Kane had been jailed in Asmaria. For instance, their current cell had bars, instead of being four walls of cold rock. There were some pallets rolled out so they could sit on something a bit suitable and not freeze as well.

Four mages stood guard outside the cell and the prisoners were ordered not to talk. The guards were to let the Guardians know anything that was said while they decided what to do. Kane was perfectly fine with sitting in silence, although, he was wishing for some water and heala. And a nap.

After a while, the Guardians retrieved them and lead them to the Capitol building to hear what they had to say. Much to Kane's surprise, there were no other people in attendance besides the Guardians, Quinn and Kailani, and the familiar-looking woman.

He stared at her, and she at him, and then he remembered. *Gethin.*

She stood before him, alive and well. She smiled with her eyes which shone brightly. She was beautiful, but not in the way that Kailani was beautiful. Gethin's was of ethereal roots.

They were sat down onto wooden chairs with no hint of gentleness. Kane groaned in protest.

Avani pointed a finger in Kane's face. "Explain yourself." Then, he crossed his arms and waited.

Kane's voice came out gravelly, "I infiltrated Aros' army, learned as much of his plans as possible, and barely escaped."

They all looked at him, waiting for more. The Guardians shared a look and then their eyes went back to him. "What else is there to say?" he asked, tired of the interrogation already.

"Who is this?" Avani pointed at Borg without breaking his gaze from Kane and then pointed at Augustus, "And what is this *filth* doing with you?"

Kane saw the fire mage's head tilt down at the insult. Kane huffed, becoming irritated. "When I got to the camp, Aros made me prove my loyalty by torturing Augustus. Aros planned to keep him just barely alive until the very end. He betrayed the promise he made to Augustus. I did what I had to do." Kane felt his cheeks warm, embarrassed by his actions now that he was saying it aloud.

"Is this true?" Gethin asked Augustus as she stepped forward, a look of genuine concern on her visage.

He nodded solemnly without looking up.

"Gethin, you cannot trust a thing he says," Avani grumbled. At the name 'Gethin', Augustus' head snapped up, eyes wide. His mouth opened as if he wanted to say something. Kane saw his eyes well up and then his head went back down. Gethin continued to look at him.

"I will be the judge of whose word I can trust, Avani," she replied.

"Do you have any idea what this man has done?" Leena interjected.

She stepped in front of Augustus and turned to the Guardians, her eyes passing over each of them. "Yes, I do know what he has done. I saw many things whilst growing inside the tree. I also know why he did the horrible things he's done. Do any of you?"

All four of them shook their heads. Gethin continued, "Fear is an excellent motivator, my friends, and Aros has shown Augustus a world where everyone he loves dies. He used that illusion to twist his mind into doing his bidding." Augustus began to sob audibly.

Kane reached over and placed a hand on his shoulder, ignoring the pain in brought him to move.

Gethin continued, "The demon king offered him a life with his family in exchange for servitude. It could have been any one of you that Aros tempted and you will never know whether you are strong enough to withstand his influence or not."

They nodded. Dihren—who'd been abnormally silent—said, "Gethin, if I may ask. What would you have us do? We can't just turn a blind eye to the crimes they've committed." He glanced at Borg. "Although, the goblin—"

"Borg," Kane interrupted the Guardian.

"Excuse me?" Dihren said.

"His name is Borg."

"Very well. Borg has done us no harm other than being in cahoots with these two."

Gethin nodded, moving around to stand behind the three on trial. Augustus still cried but his sobs had quietened. She laid her hands on his shoulders and he looked up, gasping. A yellow light emanated beneath her hands, and Kane watched with awe as the abrasions on the man's face receded. Now he just needed a shower and he'd be good as new.

She moved to Kane, repeating the same thing she'd done to Augustus. The pain relief was instant. Warmth spread throughout his body and he felt his bones begin to mend. It was unlike anything he'd ever experienced, way better than munching on heala for days. He breathed out a sigh of relief.

"Thank you," he muttered. His swimming head calmed.

"I say," Gethin began, "we listen to these gentlemen. They've been through a lot and I'm sure they have *plenty* of insider information on our common enemy. Do we have any dis-agreements?"

The Guardians shook their heads, but Kane figured that was mostly due to them not wanting to disagree with Gethin. He was thankful she was there and didn't really care why they were agreeing; he was just happy they'd done so.

"Okay," Gethin said, clapping her hands together. She pulled up a chair and gestured for everyone to do the same and said, "Now then, why don't you three tell us a story?"

Foolishness Leads to Pain

Warmth surrounded Ash's body and he heard the rhythmic knocks of what sounded like a woodpecker tapping away at the bark of a tree. Those were the two first senses that returned to him. The next was the pain of a faint, throbbing headache. He had the sensation of floating and that's because he was.

As his eyes began to crack open slowly, Ash found himself on his back, floating in a pool of water. The dual suns reminded him that he was on Tuvetal. He began to sit up in the water, the sound of a low trickle coming from behind him. He looked around; he'd been soaking in a spring of some sort. Rocks and aquatic plants adorned the pool, which made him wary. He wasn't keen on being near plants of any sort at the moment.

Behind him was the tiniest waterfall cascading over a weakly constructed dam of rocks with green moss covering their surface.

Turning back around, Ash found Raimir sitting with his legs tucked under him and his head resting on his body. Ash felt a pang of relief hit him and a knot formed in his throat. All of it was swiftly replaced with anger. He cleared his throat, the skin between his eyebrows wrinkling.

The black bird's head popped up, alerted to the noise. He rose to his feet and stretched his wings. Ash moved to climb out of the pool but Raimir's voice entered his mind, *"Don't. They're not finished."*

Ash was confused until he saw Raimir's eyes move downward. He followed the bird's gaze. There were small slug-like things slithering all over his body. Bile bubbled in his stomach.

They'll leave you once they're done, Raimir told him.

Done what?

They're removing the poison from the viperthistle.

Oh. There was a brief silence. Ash could feel Raimir's eyes watching him as he examined the slugs on his arms. He peered through the cool, clear water and could see more on his legs. That's when he realized he was stripped down to his under things. *Where are my clothes?* he asked.

They were too badly damaged to keep. They've been destroyed. A new set of clothes is being prepared for you.

By whom? The question was almost a shout. The only other thing Ash had come into contact with in this world were animals and murderous plants. Then he remembered that he was at the top of the palace and thought that something *had* to have constructed the giant structure.

I am sorry, Raimir said, and Ash saw his head droop a little. Any anger that Ash had been feeling ebbed away.

It's okay, Raimir. Penny explained everything. I forgive you.

If a giant bird could smile, Ash thought it looked like Raimir was doing so. *Looks like the slugs have done their work,* Raimir observed.

Ash saw them trekking their way down his body and off into the water. He clamored out over the edge of the pool shakily. His stomach protested with hunger. "Where can I get some food?" he asked aloud.

Follow me.

Raimir began walking away. The top of the palace was larger than he'd imagined it being. There was a square column at each of the four corners with a roof of stone placed atop them. With the size of the stones, Ash thought it defied the laws of physics, but found it more likely that this world didn't have those same laws that he was used to.

A man emerged from a hole in the center of the palace. There were stairs there leading down into the edifice. He walked with an air of superiority. It reminded Ash of Aros and he reviled the man already. But then, he noticed this man wasn't completely human.

There were twigs and sticks atop his head, crudely shaped into the form of a crown, a large verdant stone in its center. Three smaller stones of the same hue were inlaid to the left and right of the larger. He wore a sleeveless tunic that was a light brown color. The stitches and pockets were made of a dark blue material. His pants matched, tapering at the bottom.

The creature's face was like a mixture of human and monkey; light brown fur—almost orange—clung to his face and head. His ears looked more monkey, his eyes appeared more human. His arms were longer than what a man's would be and his feet were bare, although, they looked more like hands than feet.

"Welcome to Tuvetal," the man-beast said. His voice was deep and regal, commanding of respect.

"Who are you?" Ash asked, a bit more disdain in his voice than he normally would have liked. Right then, he didn't care much.

The creature shared a look with Raimir and then said, "I am Dolgatha, the Sage of Nature, King of Tuvetal." He put extra emphasis on 'King'.

"Ah," Ash said, nodding. "You're the one who almost got me killed."

Raimir's voice entered, *Be wise with what you say, Ash. The king is not to be disrespected.*

The king waved him away. "That is alright, Raimir. You needn't discourage the boy from expressing his thoughts."

So he can hear what Raimir says even in Ash's head.

"Well, was it worth it, Your Majesty?" Ash said sardonically. "Do you find me worthy?" Ash spread his arms wide and spun as he asked the question.

"I have yet to make a decision as to your worth," King Dolgatha said.

Ash dropped his arms, slapping his thighs. "What? After everything I did to get here? I made it to the palace like you wanted. What more could you want?" Ash's voice raised with each sentence and static prickled along his skin.

"Easy, boy," the king said, moving in a defensive posture. A hand went behind his back, and Ash noticed a staff strapped to him. He hadn't noticed it before. "You may want to calm down before things get out of hand."

Ash laughed at that. He was sick of people and mystical beings pissing him off. "You know, I think you're wrong. I do want things to get out of hand."

Ash no.

Ash ignored his friend. He charged the king, jumping at him with his foot out. His flying kick was easily sidestepped. The king executed a high, soaring backflip, landing on his feet and pulling the staff free from his back. King Dolgatha pulled on the staff slightly and it broke into three sections. The triple staff was connected by small chain links.

Ash summoned lightning magic into his palms, thrusting them out toward the monkey-king. Dolgatha deflected the attack with his triple staff. *Of course,* Ash thought. *The staff is impervious to my magic.*

After finding that his magic would be no use, Ash vanquished it, charging the king again. He unleashed everything he had. The young mage was nothing more than a flurry of knees and elbows, kicks and punches. None of them landed. Each blow was parried away by the triple staff. Ash thought it was quite an annoying weapon to fight against.

His energy began to fade, quicker than he'd been hoping or expecting, and King Dolgatha capitalized on it. The triple staff began battering Ash. He felt his nose break and blood gushed down his face. His arms and legs were being bruised repeatedly. In a last-ditch effort, Ash threw a straight right punch with all his force. The top and middle sections of the staff clamped down on his forearm, the monkey-man twisted his body, and the last thing Ash remembered was being flung head-first into one of the columns.

Ash opened his eyes and was met with more darkness. Stars glittered brightly above him as he floated in the pool with the healing slugs creeping along his body again. How they would heal the internal damage done by King Dolgatha, he couldn't even begin to fathom. His head hurt more than it did the first time he'd woken up in the water, but he attributed that to the swan dive he'd taken into one of the stone pillars.

"Welcome back to the land of the living," a voice said.

Ash leaned forward slowly, his head protesting against the movement. The king stood before him with a stoic look upon his face. One hand was behind his back and he held a flickering torch. It was the only light around besides that which shone down from the moon and stars.

Ash considered the moon for a moment. He could see a dim ring of gray wrapped around it.

"Can I go back to my world?" he asked, feeling utterly defeated.

"So soon?" The king's lips smirked.

"I'm done," Ash replied. "I clearly wasn't built for this." His voice had become raspy, perhaps caused by the chill of the night air.

"I disagree."

Ash squinted. How could the king disagree after what he'd done? He'd battered Ash around as if he were swatting a fly. "But you said I wasn't worthy. You know, before you kicked my butt?"

The king clicked his tongue, making a *tsk tsk* sound. "I never said you were unworthy. I said I didn't *know* if you were worthy. There's a difference."

"Not much of one," Ash argued.

"Be that as it may, I will not force you," Dolgatha said. "If you wish to go back, I will have Raimir transport you home at first light. However, if you accept to train under my tutelage, I will make you into the most formidable warrior Earth has ever seen."

At first, Ash thought to ask where his feathery friend had flown off to, but instead asked, "Accept? Are you offering?"

King Dolgatha held out the hand that had been behind him. "I am," he said. "I see great power within you, Ash. We just need to unlock it."

Ash considered it. He could easily just go back to his home and do his best to fight Aros alongside his friends. Surely there were enough Asmarians to pick up his slack.

He knew he couldn't do that.

Ash took his hand and climbed out of the pool, a slight breeze blew, sending a shiver up and down his spine. The king smiled and Ash noticed his teeth looked mostly human except for the rather sharp-looking canines.

"Very well," the king said. "I will warn you now: this will not be easy. I will not relent no matter how hard you beg, but when all is said and done, you will have become someone else, *something* else. Do you think you can handle it?"

With a nod, Ash said, "I do, King Dolgatha."

"Then let us find you some fresh clothes and a warm bed."

"A bed?" Ash asked, surprised by the notion that he wouldn't be sleeping on the hard ground, fearing for his life.

"Unless you prefer to stay out here?" the king asked.

"No way. A bed sounds fabulous."

"Good," the king turned and began walking toward the entrance at the top of the palace. "Come along, then. Tomorrow, the *real* training begins."

If the real training hadn't started yet, Ash didn't know what laid in store for him. A jolt of either fear or excitement shot through him as he followed King Dolgatha. He didn't know which and didn't care too much, he was just ready to get back home. The quicker he learned everything the Sage of Nature had to teach, the sooner he would be back with his friends. A pang of homesickness hit his heart like an arrow at the thought of Quinn, Rick, the Guardians and Gethin, and even Kane. He hoped his white-haired friend was back, if he was even coming back. No one ever really knows when you will see the people you love for the last time.

Tales to Tell

Gethin seemed to be listening with the greatest intensity, leaned forward in her chair, eyes unblinking. Kane had shared with them everything he could recall with Augustus butting in every now and then. Borg stayed silent but Kane did his best to speak on his behalf; he wanted them to know how big of a help he'd been.

"A total eclipse," Gethin repeated after Kane told her the conversation he'd overheard between Aros and the princes.

He nodded. "I'm not sure we can totally trust that, though. I mean, Aros already knew enough of our plans to lay a trap for us. He probably knew I was listening and said something false that I would find useful."

"An eclipse makes a lot of sense, though," Quinn cut in. "If the moon blots out the sun, and the Earth is plunged into darkness, I'd be willing to bet his power would increase substantially."

"I agree," Kailani added.

"Very well," Gethin said. "Then we must attack the demon and his horde before the eclipse. We move on him before he has the chance to come here."

They all nodded and a brief silence floated between them.

Kane broke it, "I just want to apologize for my actions. I know that you all," he gestured to the Guardians, "are upset with what I did before leaving. I can't really put into words how strongly I felt this was needed, and I *had* to make it believable for Aros. The best way to do that was make all of you believe I'd turned bad as well."

Bora sighed. "We understand why you did what you did. We're not happy about it, but considering all that's happened, we can't afford to stay angry with you. We need your body and mind at its best during this battle." The other three Guardians nodded.

"I also want to say," Kane went on, "the two to my right were invaluable in this operation. I would not be sitting here if not for them. I'd be either dead or imprisoned."

"Noted," Avani said. "If you have no objection, Gethin, I vote we adjourn this meeting and resume everything tomorrow. These three need rest and I know I need mine." Gethin nodded, not objecting. Then Avani pointed at Augustus, "You will not roam this island alone. Someone must keep a watchful eye on you."

"He can stay with me," Kane offered. "Borg too. I know my family's home has more than enough room to offer. Mother and father are water mages as well, so he will be tended to carefully."

"Very well," Avani said reprehensively. "You are all to meet back here in the morning."

They dismissed and left the building. The moon was shining down brightly, lighting their path down the streets of Asmaria. Borg and Augustus followed Kane toward his house. When they'd first exited, Kane tried to walk with Kailani, however, the speed at which she strode told him she wasn't in the mood for chatting.

When he walked into his home and saw his mother, the look on her face gave him a jolt of guilt. She ran to him, flinging her arms around his neck, and squeezed tightly. He chuckled against her.

"I'm sorry I made you worry," he said.

She pulled away, waving him off. "Oh, never mind that. I'm just glad you're home and safe." She glanced over his shoulder. "Who are your friends?"

Kane stepped aside so the other two could come in. "This regal little goblin is called Borg." He bowed slightly, offering her a "Madame." Kane gestured to the man. "I believe you've heard of Augustus."

Her eyes widened slightly and her skin went pale. "Of the Forbidden?" she asked.

"Yes, mother, but I assure you, his ties to the demon have been severed. In fact, I would not be standing here if not for him. He and Borg got me out of that demon's camp."

Augustus bowed to her, the same as Borg. "I am sorry for any pain I've brought your family. I am deeply ashamed of the sins I've committed against our people."

She nodded curtly. "Very well. If he's here, I can assume the Guardians have allowed it. Kane, show our guests to the rooms upstairs and then come back down. I'll fix you all something to eat."

Kane did as she asked. The look on Borg's face when he saw the massive bedroom adorned with a bed four times his size made Kane chuckle. "Never seen a bedroom like this?" he asked.

"Never slept in a bedroom at all," Borg said in a low voice.

That took Kane aback.

Back downstairs, they all joined together in fellowship. Kane's father had come out of his den where he enjoyed reading. It was nearly silent at first; only the sounds of forks on plates and mouths chomping filled the air. Borg looked like he was struggling with utensils and then gave up on using them altogether.

After their hunger was becoming sated, the group began talking together, laughing at different stories being told. Like the one Kane's father shared about when Kane had first manifested his wind magic. The white-haired kid had squealed as his body rocketed through the air, flailing about wildly.

The next morning, Kane and his new friends gathered at the Capitol building as agreed. He noticed the absence of Quinn and Kailani. He was a bit sad at that. Borg was wearing his usual clothes and dagger strapped to waist. Augustus had taken the time the night before to wash the locks from his long, matted hair. He also trimmed the hair on both head and beard.

"Let's go over all of the demon king's arsenal. Weapons, troops, anything like that," Gethin said.

Borg finally spoke up to them for the first time. "King Aros has a formidable army, My Lady. Nearly 800 beasts dredged up from the darkest pits from the earth. The most substantial of this force are the ghouls—people that the demon has reanimated, brought back to life from the dead. They are not strong or fast, but their numbers are many. Next to them are the trolls, creatures that normally reside in caves. There are a few hundred of those as well. They're big and fat, but stupid beyond belief.

"They normally don't carry weapons but their hands are strong enough to pull a person in two. The giants will be worse. They carry clubs and swords, and are several feet taller than the trolls. They come from the mountains, their skin will be thick and hard to penetrate. He has a few snake-like creatures called Leviathan, but they won't be too much of a bother. After that, there are a few wraiths and one lonely banshee. The former will not be hard to dispatch, the latter, however, is a powerful creature."

"I can attest to that," Augustus interjected. "Wench nearly ruptured my ear drums with her scream."

That seemed to surprise the group.

"As far as weapons go," Borg picked back up, "there is a sizable armory in the camp producing swords and spears, bows and arrows, and shields. I'm sure there are more things they are constructing, but to my knowledge, that is it."

"Thank you, humble goblin," Gethin said with a grateful nod. She brushed a few strands of her auburn hair behind her ear.

"What happens next?" Augustus asked. Kane watched the Guardians' faces. They didn't seem to want to answer, probably unhappy that it was he who asked.

"We prepare for battle," Dihren said definitively.

Training Begins

That first night of rest was exactly what Ash needed. He'd taken a warm bath, surprised that the palace had things like bathtubs. He had fully expected to find nothing but wilderness on the planet. The bed's sheets were silky and cool to the touch. He later learned that they'd been woven by the spiders that reside in Tuvetal.

Ash was awoken by the ringing of a bell. When he opened his eyes, King Dolgatha stood in the doorway of his room. "The time is upon us. Get up, boy." And then he was gone.

A new outfit had been laid out for him. Ash got up sluggishly and began slipping on the attire. It was similar to the king's; a soft sleeveless tunic with matching pants that tapered toward the bottom. What set his clothes apart from the king's was the color.

Ash's was mainly a deep purple and he had to appreciate that whoever stitched it together had followed the color scheme of the clothes he'd arrived in. The stitching, however, was a dull white hue. He smoothed them out after pulling them over his body. The garments fit perfectly.

Ash was dressed and ready, although, he couldn't find his shoes, which perturbed him. Shouldering his bag that had been waiting near the door, he left the room and found Dolgatha waiting.

"Do you like the clothes?" he asked quizzically.

"I do," Ash said, nodding. "But I couldn't find my shoes."

"You will find that your feet were not meant to be trapped in a rubber shoe," Dolgatha said dismissively.

Ash shrugged. "Alright. So what's first?"

Dolgatha continued down the corridor toward the stairs and said, "We climb."

And climb they did. The stairs made Ash's legs burn but it wasn't too bad, not nearly as harsh as climbing that first tree had been. The king continued walking when they reached the top of the palace. When they got to the edge, he stopped.

Pointing, the king told him, "We must journey to the top of the mountain."

Ash looked out across the expanse of jungle. Not far away was a tall mountain, taller than the palace, stretching into the clouds. "You can't be serious," Ash complained.

The king turned and held his gaze. "Life is full of trials, boy. How we handle them is what matters."

Great, he's a philosopher now, Ash thought.

As they began moving down the side of the palace, Ash asked. "Hey, where's Raimir? I haven't seen him since before you knocked me out."

"He awaits atop the mountain," Dolgatha answered. "So, if you wish to see him, you must make it there."

At the base of the mountain Ash found another set of stairs, though, these were carved into the surface of the rock. They were so steep that Ash would have been afraid of falling to his death if not for the brown vine that conveniently stretched to the top.

"I will see you up there," the king said, grabbing nearby vines with his hands and feet. "Or not," and then he was off. The monkey-man put distance between them swiftly.

"Well, here goes nothing," Ash muttered to himself, taking the vine in hand.

Several times on his way up the mountain Ash had almost fallen. His feet would slip beneath a patch of moss or on a slick step. His knuckles turned white from gripping the vine so tightly. His muscles burned and ached; a few times he had to stop to let the lactic acid dissipate a bit.

After what he figured had been several hours, Ash finally crested the top of the mountain. His new shirt was wet with sweat, his feet screamed in pain, unaccustomed to not having padding between themselves and the ground. His fingers throbbed as blisters threatened to explode, and his muscles were cramping. The mage flopped onto his back, sucking in air as if it would soon run out.

Welcome, Raimir said in his mind. *Easy climb, yes?*

Is that sarcasm? At a time like this? Ash thought back to him. A slight chuckle entered his brain.

Ash drank deeply from the water skin he'd freed from inside his gear bag. King Dolgatha stood in the center of a circle of medium-sized stones, no bigger than a foot high or wide. He waited patiently with his hands behind his back. A small stream trickled nearby, cascading down one side of the mountain.

Ash stood, looking out over the planet. It was so vast and beautiful. As if reading his mind, Raimir asked, *Beautiful, isn't it?*

It really is, Ash replied.

The circumstances that have brought you here are most unfortu-nate, but I'm glad you've been able to see my home.

As am I.

"Are you rested? Ready?" the king asked.

Ash turned. "I guess that depends on what I should be ready for."

Dolgatha began pacing around the inside of the stone circle. "There is but one way to enter a higher level of strength or power." Ash said nothing, and the king went on, "Pain. Pain breeds strength as weakness breeds pain. When you leave this world, you will have known pain."

"I've already known pain," Ash said, not a hint of sarcasm in his voice.

"Join me in the circle and tell me of this pain."

Ash stepped forward warily, suspicious that the king could be tricking him. Dolgatha appeared to be waiting so Ash told him all that he'd been through. He began by recanting the story of being abandoned, his father killing his mother and leaving him there. He told him about Rick and how angry he'd been at the man for never letting him leave their home, fearing for his safety.

When Ash got to the moment of being possessed by Aros and killing Brandr, a knot formed in his throat. He choked it back down. Ash told him about Draven and how foolish he'd been to let his emotions over a girl get the better of him. Throughout all of it, the king listened and never once looked away from Ash.

"Your life is indeed filled with a lot of pain," the king said, "and that pain has made you strong enough to get here. No ordinary person could have accomplished all that you have thus far."

Ash didn't feel like he'd accomplished all that much to begin with.

"Despite all that, however, you must become stronger to destroy this beast you face."

"Why don't you just fight him?" Ash asked. "I can already tell you're one of the strongest people—or whatever—that I've ever met."

He chuckled at that. "It is not my place to fight the demon. It is yours. 'Boy born of a lightning bolt.'" He quoted the last part. "You must do this for yourself and your people."

King Dolgatha unstrapped the staff from his back and laid it aside. Ash glanced toward Raimir. *Good luck* was all the giant black bird said.

Ash readied himself for another fight, bringing his hands up defensively. The king turned back to face him, one hand behind his back and the other rising in front of him. His four fingers pointed at Ash and curled in a quick, 'come here' motion as he said, "Let's see what you've got."

Jasper

The training field was filled with more Asmarians than Quinn had ever seen all at once. It seemed like the entire island had gathered. They sat in the grass, waiting for Gethin to speak. She conversed quietly with the Guardians before finally turning to address the crowd of warriors.

"Thank you all for coming," she began. "There are dark days ahead of us and we must all work together if we are to win this fight. As many of you know, I will die before it's all done." Murmurs fluttered around but it wasn't the uproarious chaos that had incurred the last time she mentioned it in front of everyone.

"I understand that most of you have come to believe that I am the source of your magic. You fear that in losing me, you shall also lose your magic. As the Great Tree, you all would have given your lives to prevent my demise and I thank you for your love and loyalty. However, I must set the record straight." She paused and Quinn held her breath, unsure of what was coming.

"I am not the granter of the magic that fills you. You will not lose your power simply at my death. Magic flows within each and every one of you, and as long as your bloodlines continued, so will the life of our magic." A collective breath of relief was released.

"This beautiful island, Asmaria, which you all have known as home will be fine as well. You brave warriors and your ancestors have protected me for thousands of years, and now I must return that favor." Cheers rang out through the Asmarians.

Avani walked up next to Gethin. "We understand that many of you were not born with magic in your blood, however, we still need you to fight alongside us. *The world* needs you." His voice rose with the next sentence, not out of anger, but with determination. "It needs your swords, your spears, your arrows!" Cheers were getting louder and Quinn found herself joining in, fist pumping in the air.

"I tell you, Asmarians," Avani continued shouting. He turned and grabbed something from a table and hefted it into the air. The point of the Bane of Darkness aimed at the sky. "We now have a way to destroy the demon king, Aros!" The roars intensified even further as the Sword of Pescalon gleamed.

Quinn saw Gethin beaming at everyone. "Let us begin!" the deity shouted, lifting her hands toward the sky.

Swords clattered against shields and arrows zipped through the air and into targets as the preparation for the coming battle ensued. Leena trained the water mages, showing them tips and tricks that she'd learned over the years. She taught them how to increase their concentration to hold liquid forms for longer. The Guardian didn't spend too much time with Quinn, seeing as she was the only mage capable of turning water into ice.

Quinn walked around, lending a hand where need be, giving the mages tips of her own. She saw her parents figuring out which weapons suited them best. Rick was sparring with a longsword in one hand, shield strapped to the other. The Asmarian he faced was roughly the same size, but Rick was besting him with each bout. Quinn thought how proud Ash would be of him if he could see him now. Then, a longing pang hit her gut and she felt sick. She missed him and his silly demeanor badly.

Throughout the day, Quinn learned that, for the first time in years, the old armory was back in use. The furnaces were ignited and weapons were being crafted alongside armor. The Guild probably wouldn't wear any for the most part, but the Asmarians without magic would benefit from it.

Jasper Hawthorn was a young earth mage, and although he was a member of the Guild, he was often overlooked by his peers. Jasper was deaf, born that way, and none of the other mages had ever learned how to use sign language. Only his parents had taken the time to do so. Jasper had learned how to read lips very well over the years.

Despite that, he was fairly easy-going and thankful for all he had. He wasn't exceptionally powerful like the white-haired Kane Volorium. He wasn't terribly intelligent or athletic either. He'd never been chosen to go on a quest of any sort by the Guardians.

Jasper admired Ash and his friends more than anyone he'd met in his thirteen years of life. They probably didn't even know Jasper existed, considering he had no real way to communicate with them. He was there when Ash had first arrived in Asmaria on the giant bird's back. He was there when Ash inadvertently killed Brandr. He remembered how Ember had formed a mob to stand against the other Guardians and could recall the moment the Great Tree was cured.

The young boy just wanted to be like them. He yearned for an opportunity to show everyone that being deaf was not the disability they think it is. His being able to hear wouldn't make him greater at performing magic.

One day, he told himself. *One day I will prove my worth.*

Jasper continued to practice, ripping the ground up in large chunks and slamming those chunks into targets. His brow beaded with sweat and furled with determination to become the strongest mage possible.

Phase Two

"Once you land a blow on me, your training can advance to the next stage," King Dolgatha had told Ash.

Thus far, Ash had only come minorly close to punching him. Several times Ash had thrown a furious combination of punches and kicks, all defected by the king's limbs; he wasn't even using his triple staff anymore. More than once Dolgatha had narrowly avoided a punch to the face, turning his shoulder and grabbing Ash's arm. As he put his back to the mage, he bent at the waist, never letting go of Ash's wrist and arm, and tossed him over his shoulder without mercy. That always made Ash's ribs feel like they'd cracked.

Within the sparring circle Ash had agreed not to use his lightning magic on the king since the magic-impervious triple staff lay too far away for Dolgatha to protect himself with.

It had been roughly five days since they started the task of turning Ash into a great warrior. At the start of each day, Ash was required to climb the stairs of the mountain and spar with the king. It took four of those days for his bare feet and toes to get callused enough that climbing the steps no longer hurt as bad. It still strained the muscles in his arms and legs to no end, but not as bad as the first day. At the end of those days, Raimir was allowed to fly Ash back down to the palace where he would soak in the healing pool for a few hours, eat some stew that King Dolgatha had prepared, and sleep for as long as possible. Ash didn't know what was in the stew—and was too afraid to ask—but it was divine.

Now, on the sixth day of fighting atop the mountain, something clicked within Ash. Dolgatha had not thrown a single blow unless in defense. Ash would throw a strike at him which was parried or ducked or dodged. Sometimes his opponent would parry and then return with a strike of his own, or just simply created distance between them again.

Ash threw a few combinations and received a kick to the stomach as his prize. He began imitating the man-beast's stance: knees slightly bent and body angled toward him, both arms stretching toward him with the palms up and fingers pressed slightly together.

He knew Dolgatha noticed by the smirk that twitched at his lips. Then he said, "Ah, learning are we?"

Ash didn't answer, shuffling closer to the king instead. When their front hand's fingers were nearly touching, Dolgatha finally struck first. With a whirling motion, Ash swung his front arm in a circle which blocked the fist heading for his nose. The punch missed obtusely and Ash wasted no time. He shot a straight right punch that landed squarely in the king's chest. A "hmpf" escaped the king as he was pushed back several inches.

Ash breathed hard. It took him nearly six and a half days to figure out how to land a punch on King Dolgatha and he was worn. He looked at Dolgatha who was smiling brightly.

"Well done," the king said. "Now we can move on to the next

task, although once we start, you may prefer the sparring."

That sat in Ash's gut like a rock. What was next? He couldn't imagine it getting more difficult. "What, are you going to make me run across the jungle again? Fight a gorilla the size of the trees?"

The king chuckled. "No, nothing that serious. It's more boring, really, but it will make you stronger."

Ash was ready. "Okay, let's do it then."

"Tomorrow. You have earned a day of respite. You will meet me up here at the same time."

There goes the brief thought of not having to climb those cursed stairs anymore.

King Dolgatha climbed down the mountain as Ash mounted the giant bird. As he launched, his voice entered Ash's mind. *I'm proud of you, Ash. I want you to know that.*

I haven't really done much, Ash commented. *I only hit the guy once and he was probably going easy on me.*

Raimir chuckled, *Yes, but if he went all out, you would die.* That gave Ash pause. Is the king *really* that strong? *Nevertheless, you struck him without any help or instruction. That itself is no easy feat. King Dolgatha is a valiant warrior and has never lost a battle.*

Wow, Ash marveled to himself. He still didn't feel like he'd done much, but it was a good feeling to have gotten past the first part of his training with the monkey-man.

"I've been meaning to ask you," Ash began, stretching his aching limbs on top of the mountain. "Where do you come from?"

"I—like all those who reside in Tuvetal—were born out of necessity," Dolgatha replied. "Your planet's history is deep, and there are many more planets throughout the cosmos that desire help from time to time." Dolgatha continued after seeing the confused look on Ash's face.

"Picture it like this: each planet is a living being. Just like all living things, the planets require balance or they will perish. When one of these planets is on the verge of collapse, a new creature is born on Tuvetal. Now, there are many creatures in my world who are not meant to be protectors of worlds, they merely sustain those of us who are."

"So, you don't know where you came from exactly?" Ash asked.

"Not exactly, no," the king agreed. "Nor do we find it to matter. We know what our purpose is and that is enough."

Ash thought that was beautiful in its own way. The creatures on Tuvetal didn't need to worry about anything besides answering the call to action—aiding planets in their survival—whenever it arises.

"Are you ready to begin phase two?"

"I am." Ash was determined to do whatever it takes to become stronger.

"Do as I," Dolgatha said. He squatted deeply with his feet out wide. He stretched his arms out directly in front of him with the index finger and thumb on each hand creating an "L" shape. Ash copied him.

When he'd gotten into position, the king stood walking around Ash slowly and inspecting his form. Ash felt his legs begin to wobble after a minute.

"Good," King Dolgatha observed. "Don't move." He turned and walked away, coming back a few seconds later with a handful of smooth stones, almost like the ones used in a spa.

The king began placing them, one at a time, along Ash's arms.

He started at the wrist, placing one, then another. Ash had four of the stones on his arms when they started to tremble along with his legs. A stone fell and Ash looked down. A force hit him in the ribs suddenly, knocking him to the hard ground.

When he recovered, King Dolgatha had his staff in hand. Ash never saw him retrieve it. The mage winced and rubbed the throbbing ribs.

"Again!" King Dolgatha ordered.

Ash rose slowly and got back into the squatted stance. The king began placing the rocks on him again. He was able to keep them balanced on his wrists longer the second time, however, they fell and he was smacked with the staff again.

Leviathan

Knowing that Aros planned to attack Asmaria the day of the total solar eclipse was helpful, but they had to do some research to find out when that would be. The news spread that the eclipse would be in fifteen days. That didn't give them much time to do anything. The Asmarians were taking shifts between training and working and resting.

Kane had finally gotten Kailani to talk to him after a few days of the cold shoulder and silent treatment. She'd come around and fallen into his arms once again. He'd given her a kiss on the forehead, apologizing over and over. "Out of all the people I hurt, your pain has tortured me the most," he told her.

Now, they were working on building boats. Twenty large vessels were to be constructed and, with the help of the Atlanteans, construction was going smoothly. They had to fell many trees which made most of the Asmarians feel bad; they loved nature, especially that which grew on the island. Each time a tree was knocked down, the crew would be sure to relocate every critter they could find that would be affected by it. Wind mages would hold the tree aloft, keeping it from smashing down other plants and animals unnecessarily.

There were only ten more boats to go and twelve days left before the eclipse. As the time wore on, Kane became more and more worried that Ash wouldn't return in time. What would happen if he showed up too late, or what if he had already been killed somehow? Kane didn't like to think about that.

Kane observed Borg and Augustus working tirelessly on the tasks at hand. The goblin was either always hefting heavy building materials for the boats or teaching a youth how to handle a dagger. He was stout enough to carry a ten-foot log on his shoulder and swift with a blade.

Augustus was always under a watchful eye; the Guardians were determined to not let him hurt anyone. However, unless the man was playing at some grand cous, Kane figured he would never return to the demon king. He was on their side until the end. The fire mage could be found hammering away on the wooden ships or teaching other mages how to wield flames. He, alongside Dihren, were creating a lethal batch of mages. Kane even saw the two men joking around with each other a few times.

The banshee—who goes by the name, Kagni—wasn't all too ready to join the dark lord's evil vendetta. She was the last off her kind and old, very old. Once a beautiful nature spirit, she had been corrupted by dark magic, but she could still remember what it was like to not be a banshee.

Kagni's entire coven of spirits became banshees due to her mistakes. The rest of them had all died and she knew her time was nearly up. Cursed to be a banshee, and cursed again to watch her family die one by one. That's why she joined King

Aros. She didn't care what happened to him, herself, or this accursed world. The world had left her to rot in the depths of the earth. Kagni made peace with her situation. Then he came, promising a life of grandeur. Kagni knew she would probably never see it, but the demon king made a compelling point. She had nothing to lose.

She watched him silently, her voice much too powerful to use for small talk, as he performed yet more dark magic to release a monster from the pits. He laughed maniacally as his shadows wafted from his body and soaked into the soil, turning it black. She could smell the acidity from the ruined dirt. A hole began to form, small at first, and then widening. She mirrored Aros as he began stepping back away from it.

The dirt continued to cave in, the hole enlarging, until it was at least 50 meters wide. Whatever he is awakening, she knew it was bad. He said a word in the old language, the one that was used at the dawn of creation.

"Zhyrvak," he uttered.

"Zhyrvak," again and again he repeated the word, his voice a crescendo. The word meant 'rise', spoken in a tongue that was more powerful than anything.

The ground began to quake and Kagni took a few more tentative steps back, although Aros did not. A form began to emerge from the crater that had developed. The shape of curled horns atop a massive head came first. Two gargantuan, clawed hands gripped the rim of the pit and the beast pulled itself free.

Kagni, as dark and vile as she may be, was terrified by just looking at it. How they could lose this war she couldn't fathom. The creature stood at least 150 meters tall; its head was nearly touching the clouds. The eyes were blacker than black and it had no lips, just a wide mouth with rows of razor-sharp teeth. Each tooth had to be bigger than the banshee.

She stared at it in awe. Aros looked at her. "Marvelous, isn't he?"

Kagni nodded. "What is it, My Lord?"

"That," he said gleefully, "is the Leviathan."

Then he let loose a tentacle of shadow that sailed through the air until smashing into the giant beast's face. He was showing him where to attack. Their enemy believes Aros' entire army will be coming for them, but she knew this was a ruse. It would only be the Leviathan who was going to destroy them. The creature's muscled body rippled from the impact of its steps as he marched towards the sea.

Make Savage the Body

The more that wicked staff clashed with Ash's body, the harder his body became. It took him a while to not drop the initial four stones that was being balanced on his wrists. He'd been whacked by the king at least a hundred times, and with each strike, he grew stronger. Eventually, Ash was able to hold the stones steady, but then Dolgatha added more.

He was up to four on each wrist and four on the top of his head. He'd been holding the pose for hours with his eyes closed. He found it easier to concentrate if he didn't know exactly what was going on around him.

"Good," Dolgatha murmured. "Very good, Ash. I believe you are ready for the next phase."

"Thank you," Ash said, opening his eyes and standing up. He didn't even feel the stones bouncing off the top of his feet. "What's next?"

"I teach you how to fight."

"I'm pretty good at that already," Ash said coyly.

"Not good enough."

They began with Ash shadowing his movements. They were in the deep squat with their hands and arms moving around like fluid. It reminded Ash of something he'd watched about Tai Chi on TV. It was a slow, methodical movement and Ash failed to see how it would translate to fighting, but he said nothing and instead trusted the process.

"Continue the form," Dolgatha said as he walked around, watching him.

"Seems like this phase is going to be less hitting me, yes?" Ash asked.

"Yes, but it requires more focus." A subtle hint to tell Ash to be quiet. He did.

This went on for several days and Ash's concern of not making it back to Asmaria in time increased. When he raised the concern to Dolgatha, the Sage of Nature told him dismissively, "Time here moves differently. When you return to your world, you will find that not all that much time has passed for your friends."

Ash took him at his word and continued to do everything he said. King Dolgatha had begun smacking him with the staff again while Ash performed the fluid motions of whatever fighting form the king had shown him. The force with which he used to strike Ash was less than when he'd been balancing the stones, or so he thought. What *really* happened was that his body had toughened to the point that he was feeling less and less pain.

Within a few more days, Ash had completed the phase after landing several strikes against Dolgatha. Ash did his best to combine the new style with any of the old boxing and grappling techniques he already knew. He still figured that the old sage wasn't giving his all, but Ash was able to land more strikes and avoid taking as much damage as all the previous sparring matches.

"I want you to close your eyes and summon the magic inside you. Let it rest in your palms," King Dolgatha told him.

They sat across from each other with legs crossed and palms facing the blue sky. Ash did what he said and could feel the crackle of lightning in his hands as it formed.

"What did you feel just before the lightning formed?"

Ash's eyebrows furled. "I'm not sure." The strike came instantly. The staff smashed the top of his head and Ash felt his anger flare. He hardly flinched from the blow.

"Again."

Ash let the magic disappear, starting the process over. He conjured it, this time paying special attention to anything he might feel prior to its formation. He noticed something. "I felt it in my chest," he said.

"Yes, that's it," the monkey-king said with a cheery voice. "Mages have always believed their magic to come from their hands, but in reality, it comes from the heart."

"So, you've known other mages?" Why that was the question he asked, Ash wasn't sure.

The king chuckled, "Of course." He said it as if it was supposed to be obvious. "Now, what this tells us is that you can spread the magic to any part of your body. You must learn to control it so finely that you can conjure it to your entire being, down to the last cell."

"That sounds like a lot of work," Ash blew out a breath.

"Indeed it is, so I suggest you get to it."

Ash opened his eyes when he heard the king's feet scuffling along the mountain. "Where are you going?"

The sage walked to the edge of the mountain and, turning over his shoulder, he said, "This task you must do alone. Find it within yourself to complete this part of the journey. Your limits are set within your mind; surpass them. I will know once you've done so." And with that, he fled the mountain along with Raimir. Ash was alone again.

"Well," he said, surprisingly upbeat, "no sense in wasting time." He closed his eyes and began searching within himself a way to better control his magic. For the first time in probably all his life, he truly believed he could do something great on his own. He was entirely confident that he'd be able crush the task at hand.

Ash didn't sleep; he didn't have time for that. Every time he tried to spread the lightning to a different part of him, it would just fizzle out and he was becoming increasingly frustrated. How many days had passed? The rumble in his stomach reminded him it had been three days and three nights. Ash didn't bother eating or resting and his body was hating him for it.

"Just a little nap," he whispered to himself as he slumped over and closed his eyes. He'd lost all energy and strength.

When he awoke, he found it to be night; the moon was hanging up high and the stars were twinkling brightly. Without missing a beat, he began again. Closing his eyes and conjuring the lightning to his palms, imagining it spreading up his arms. Finally, as if he'd been pulling a heavy object with a rope, it broke free. He inhaled sharply as the purple arcs began racing up his arms, then vanished.

He did it again, imagining he was pulling it all over the rest of his body. He rewarded himself that night.

There was a small jungle rat of some sort that had climbed the mountain and was drinking from the stream. Ash killed it with a single bolt of lightning from his fingertip. It died instantly and he cooked it over a fire. He might have felt somewhat ashamed eating something like that, but his stomach didn't care what he was eating. He took another nap and awoke the following morning to continue practicing.

"I see you've figured it out," King Dolgatha observed. Ash sat with his back to him, amethyst arcing around his entire body like a thin layer of electrical armor.

"It would seem as though I have," Ash said. "Am I ready to go home yet?"

"Not quiet, but very close."

Ash stood and turned, not bothering to kill the magic. It flowed through him brightly and his energy felt higher than ever. Fatigue ran from him. "What's next then?"

"You must learn to increase the lethality of your magic," he answered.

"Like how?"

"You will make yourself into lightning. You will be one with it, not apart from it. You will use it to power your strikes and quicken your legs. When it is over, you shall be able to call it from the skies." He glanced up at the last word.

"The skies?" Ash repeated.

"Yes," Dolgatha nodded. "The magic that you mages control is *always* more powerful when the real thing is manipulated. The lightning you conjure comes from your being, not nature. That is why earth mages are so powerful. It is always readily available and they don't even have to create it from nothing."

"I see," Ash said, nodding. What the king was saying resonated within him. "Let's get started then."

Training Complete

With the ships complete, the Asmarians and Atlanteans began loading them with armor, weapons, and any other provision they could think of. There were barrels filled with water and food. Kane couldn't help but think how much this made them look like the pirates in the old books he used to peruse.

Kane left the ships to walk back to the training field with Augustus and Borg to see if there were any other weapons or supplies to haul. They were walking onto the field as other mages were leaving with arms full of weapons and such, when a familiar loud crack echoed around. Kane stopped and began looking around. He spotted Quinn doing the same.

"What was that?" Borg said.

"I think Ash may have returned," Kane muttered, looking around the sky. Then it appeared; a shape that grew larger and larger. It was a bird, Kane could see that from the flapping wings, but it was much bigger and darker than he remembered Raimir being. Kane could see someone sitting atop the bird's back.

Ash had completed the final phase of his training in around a week of Tuvetal time, and was returning home with a whole new arsenal at his disposal. He and Raimir cracked through the sky, splitting through different dimensions.

Don't think I'll ever get used to that, Ash transmitted to his friend.

I fear that may be the last time you travel with me through space and time, Ash.

What? Ash hadn't ever considered their companionship would end.

After this war is over I will return to my home, and you will stay here. That is the way things must be.

Sadness flooded Ash at that notion. *Well, I'll certainly never forget you.*

Nor I you.

Asmaria was growing in shape and Ash found himself on the verge of tears. He was elated—to say the least—to be back with his family and friends. Excitement grew in him as he thought about hugging all of them. He began wondering if Kane had returned, if he was going to, anyway. But then he was relieved to find he didn't have to wonder for long.

That white hair he would recognize anywhere. His friend was looking up at him standing next to two others. *Good,* Ash thought to himself. *They let him return after all.*

Then his world was rocked as he looked more closely at the two people next to his best friend. One, a short ugly creature that Ash was unsure what to call. The other, a man Ash wished to kill for the pain and suffering he'd brought him. His father. "Fly upside down," he shouted over the wind at Raimir.

Kane waved at his friend, finally seeing him as the bird flipped over and began flying upside down. Ash fell from the bird's back, at least fifty feet in the air. The ground would most likely kill him if he hit. Kane's hands flared wide as he was about to conjure the wind to capture his friend. Just before though, another crack of lightning echoed around the field. A purple flash lit up the day sky and Ash had vanished. The bolt of purple struck the ground, sending bits of dirt up into the air.

When the dust settled, Kane saw Ash on the ground only thirty feet away. The boy was on one knee with his head facing down, his fists dug into the soil. Lightning charged around his entire body and he had sunken into the ground several inches. When Ash stood, he had to pull his fists and feet free from the dirt. The bird landed swiftly behind him.

"Whoa!" Kane shouted, walking forward with his arms wide. "That was awesome, man!"

"What," Ash growled, "is he doing here?" he pointed at Augustus who stood a few feet behind Kane with an unreadable expression.

"Look, it's not what it looks—" before he could finish his sentence, a lasso of purple shot from Ash's hand and snaked around his father. The man yelled in agony and writhed from the pain.

"Stop it, Ash!" Kane shouted as Quinn got closer. She'd been running to him just before the lasso lashed out.

"You!" he yelled, looking at Kane. A sphere of purple was forming in Ash's hand; he pulled his arm back and was about to hurl it when Gethin came from nowhere. She jumped in front of him and stared him in the face.

"Enough," Kane heard her say. Ash's magic faded almost instantly.

As if this new control and strength of Ash wasn't terrifying enough, Kane also noticed that what he'd just done was effortless. The aura emanating from his was intense. The wind mage wondered if this was the same boy that he once called his best friend.

Ash Gets a Surprise

"What is he doing here?" Ash asked again, this time to Gethin.

"He is on our side now," she replied.

Ash's hands went to the side of his head and he turned in circles saying, "No, no, no. Don't you know what he's done? Don't you understand all the pain that he's brought me—brought to every Asmarian?"

"I'm well aware of the crimes he's committed."

"Then why?" Ash shouted, throwing his hands up in exasperation. "Why would you let him stay here? What did the Guardians have to say about this?"

Gethin said, "They were less than excited to allow him refuge here."

"And you ignore them? Let him poison us with his presence?"

She put a hand on his shoulder then. "I understand your anger and frustration at this situation. I know it will be difficult to let this go. Everything happens for a reason, Ash, and your father is here for a *reason*. Everyone deserves a second chance to prove themselves. You, of all people, should know that."

He thought she could be referring to any number of failures he'd had over the last couple of years. Ash closed his eyes and tried to let the anger melt away, but it stayed. "Fine. I'll be cooperative. But I will not forgive you." He shouted the last words at Augustus.

Ash walked past Gethin and sauntered up to his father, stopping just a few inches away. Not a hint of fear in him as there would have been in the past. He whispered so that only he and Augustus could hear, "They may have forgiven and forgotten what you've done to us, but I will never forget what you did to my mother."

At that, Augustus' knees buckled and planted themselves in the ground. He sobbed quietly. Then, he looked up and muttered, "I'm so sorry, son."

"You don't get to call me that," Ash snapped. "I have a dad. His name is Rick Hampton." Then Ash turned to Kane and moved to get in his face as well. Kane recoiled slightly, a look of apprehension on his face.

Ash found himself more relieved that Kane was back than angry at his seemingly fake betrayal. He smiled, "So, you're back huh?"

Kane sighed. "That I am. Back with friends, as you can see." He gestured to Augustus and Borg. "Remind me to tell you the whole story later. I want to hear all about your training with Raimir too. That superhero landing? Wicked."

Ash chuckled. "Sounds great, but I'm pretty tired. I think I'm going to go find Rick and let him know I'm back. Any idea where he'd be?"

"Probably at your house resting. He's been working himself ragged on the ships."

"Ships?" Ash asked, confounded.

Kane chuckled, "A lot has happened since you've been away; we're sailing out to take the fight to Aros in a few days."

"Guess I better get some rest in those few days then."

Ash gave Quinn a quick hug, told her he'd missed her a lot, and that they would talk more later. At the moment, however, he was feeling fatigued from the teleportation via Raimir. Moving at the speed of lightning didn't help to ease the fatigue either.

Raimir gave him a lift back to his house where he found Rick napping on the couch. When Ash woke him, the man was very surprised to see his adoptive son standing before him. He jumped up and threw his arms around him immediately.

He pulled back, saying, "Wow, kid, you been working out?"

Ash laughed at that. "Yeah, something like that."

"You feel strong." He glanced down. "And where are your shoes?"

"I don't really wear them anymore."

Ash launched into the whole story, telling him of everything he'd been through. Rick's facial expression changed several times throughout the story, moving from worry to awe to joy.

"I'm proud of you," Rick told him, hugging him tightly once again.

"Did you know Augustus is here?" Ash asked.

"I guess you saw him then," Rick noted. "Yes, I knew. I spoke with him a couple of times as well. He approached me, thanked me for taking care of you and keeping you safe all those years. I really do think he feels remorse, though I know it won't be easy for you to forgive him."

"To say the least," Ash muttered.

"I want you to try, Ash. Holding on to anger and all the negative feelings you have towards him is not healthy. I *know* how hard it can be to let it all go, trust me. I'm just asking you try, if not for me or anyone else, do it for yourself."

Ash nodded. "You kind of remind me of King Dolgatha. He was always saying wise things like that."

Then Ash promptly flung himself onto his bed and passed out, not wanting to think about anything else for the rest of the day or night.

The following day, feeling much better after having rested, Ash went to look for his estranged father. He wasn't happy or excited at the prospect, but rather dreaded to be in close proximity with the man. He found him with Kane and the creature he'd learned was a goblin named Borg.

"Can I speak with Augustus alone?" Ash asked, making a point to not call him his dad or father or anything like that.

Augustus stepped away and they walked further up the beach, away from the large boats. Ash saw Thaoc carrying a large wooden barrel on one shoulder and gave him a wave to which the giant man returned.

When they were far enough away from prying ears, Ash said, "I guess I'll start." Then he let out a deep breath. "Like I said yesterday, I do not intend to forget the things you've done. Despite all the crap you put me through, though, I will try to forgive you."

The man looked like he was going to break down again, but then he steadied himself and stood a bit straighter. Ash continued, "I will not call you dad or father, but only Augustus. You will not call me son, only Ash. You don't deserve that title. Only one man has earned that."

Augustus nodded. "I understand and agree to that. I know that I can never atone for the things that I've done, but that doesn't mean I won't do my darndest. Maybe when this is all over and Aros is dead, we can get to know each other a little better. I can tell you more about your mother." The word mother escaped his lips with a shutter.

Ash took deep breaths to calm the anger that arose from him speaking of her. "Maybe," was all he could get out.

Augustus reached into a pocket of his pants and pulled out a small enveloped. "She gave this to me. It's a letter that she wrote for you in case anything ever happened to her. I didn't know what I would do to her back then." Silent tears worked down his cheeks.

Ash reached out and took it with shaking hands. He didn't know what to say. He left the man on the beach and walked into the jungle. Sitting atop Sunset Crest—the giant rock that peaked over the treetops—he pulled the letter free of the envelope. It had tan splotches all over it and looked a bit weathered. He unfolded it slowly, careful not to tear the paper. He began reading.

Dear Ash,

If you're reading this then something has happened to me. I want you to know how much I love you. Just look up at the sky. The vastness of the sky does not hold a match to the amount of love I have for you, my baby boy. Your father loves you too, but I think I've got him beat (don't tell him I said so). If there is ever a time in your life when you're feeling down on yourself, or feeling like you're not good enough, I want you to stop and close your eyes, take a deep breath, and shake those feelings away. You will always be good enough, Ash. You will grow to be a brave man, I just know it. I know it in my heart that you will be a hero one day and I am already so proud of you. Never forget that no matter where I may be, no

matter how far apart we are, I will always be with you. Look to your heart and that's where I'll be. I love you, my son.
   -Love Mom.

Raindrops began peppering the page. No, those were his tears. Ash couldn't contain them no matter how hard he tried. He moved the page from beneath his face so that it wouldn't get ruined. The tears streamed down his cheeks like rivers. Clouds formed overhead and he could hear the thunder roll, feel it in his chest.

He heard feet scuffle behind him and turned. The man he was supposed to hate was there. The man he should want to rip apart, to kill, as he'd done to his mother. But Ash found that he didn't want to do any of that. Ash stood and fell into the arms of his father, sobs muffled against the man's chest. Augustus stroked Ash's hair, "Shh, shh."

Ash didn't know how long he'd stayed there, but he knew it had been a long time. When he felt all cried out, he back away and wiped his face fervently. Augustus wore a sad smile.

"Anything you want to say to me?" Augustus asked. "Threaten me or something? It might make you feel better."

Ash shook his head. "No, she wouldn't want that. I just have one thing to say."

"What?"

Ash looked him dead in the eyes. "Let's go kill the bastard that tore our family apart."

Something Wicked This Way Comes

Ash sat up in his bed; the alarm bell that alerted the Asmarians to an imminent attack was ringing loudly. How long had it been since the bell had been struck? Rick rushed into his room. "Hear that?"

Ash nodded, ripping the blankets away. He threw on the pants and tunic he'd gotten from King Dolgatha.

This wasn't supposed to be happening yet. According to Kane's information, Aros' army was supposed to attack the island in another couple of days when the total solar eclipse was happening.

Rick put on his shoes and then they left the house together.

Something is coming, Raimir said, standing there on the street. *Something big.*

Ash and Rick hopped on his back and flew into the sky, looking to see where the most people were congregating. *Looks like they're gathered on the beach,* Ash transmitted. They dived down to the other people. Rick jumped off and ran for some armor and weapons. Gethin and the Guardians were ordering people around.

Ash ran over and yelled over the ruckus, "What is going on?"

Avani answered, "The Atlanteans warned us that something

large was stomping through the sea headed this way. We're taking the ships to fight against whatever it is. Pick a boat and climb aboard; it's time to see what new skills you've learned."

Ash grinned. "I'll be in the air." Then he climbed back on Raimir and conjured the magical bow into his hand.

Let's go scout this thing out, Ash said.

Raimir agreed and they launched from the beach. Ash looked back to see the entire Guild piling into the ships along with various Asmarians. Looks like their mettle will be tested early.

A few hundred meters away from the island they found the monster. Ash could just barely make it out from beneath the water. It's massive frame was causing the ocean to swirl and churn with each step it took. He could see horns on its head and that was about it.

He asked Raimir to go back so that he could let them know what he saw, and that's what they did. Gethin shook her head after listening. "I don't believe it," she muttered.

"What? What is this thing?" Dihren asked. All of them looked afraid.

"It's the Leviathan," she said, barely audible. "I didn't think he knew about that monster. This is a creature as old as the Earth. We are in grave danger."

"What do you recommend we do?" Leena inquired.

Gethin nodded, seeming to snap out of the fear. "Leave a few ships here to patrol around the island, just in case. Have the best mages venture out to meet the Leviathan. We will need a variety of element wielders on each vessel; some to manipulate the waters and some to conjure the winds in our sails. Those not steering or maneuvering their boats will attack with all they have. With luck, we will live through this to see tomorrow."

Ash felt his rage building and decided he would not listen to any more of what was being said. He ran to Raimir and climbed on the bird's back. They flew away again. This time, the Leviathan's head was sticking up out of the water. Raimir floated by and Ash began launching electrified arrows from the Atlantean bow at the top of its head. They just sputtered upon contact with its hide.

"This is no good," he shouted. "Get me closer!"

Raimir circled down lower and Ash stood on his back. He conjured magic into is palms and unleashed it on the beast. Still, nothing happened. Dread filled his soul. How were they going to beat this thing?

Kane thought Borg looked petrified. The Leviathan was closing in on the island. It's gargantuan physique was rising steadily from the water. Kane could see the Atlanteans attacking its lower body from the ocean, however, it didn't seem to notice them. He knew the city of Atlantis was being smashed by the giant's feet. He just hoped they were able to get out of its way in time. He thought to look for Kailani, but then remembered she was not someone who needed a hero to save her. She was a strong warrior, not a helpless damsel.

"I've got to take this fight to the air," Kane told Borg. "Either stay here and help people defend the island, or climb on a boat, although I'd hurry if I were you. Looks like they're leaving." The ships were beginning to pull away. Kane saw Gethin run off into the jungle and found it odd that she would leave the fight, although he suspected she had good reason.

Kane watched Borg run to a ship, still looking horrified, and then summoned the magic that allowed him to fly. He found

Ash flying around and landed next to him, startling the boy.

"Anything working yet?" Kane asked.

Ash shook his head. "Its skin seems to be so thick that my lightning just bounces right off."

Kane nodded. "Let me try." He jumped from the bird, diving towards the monster. When he was eye level with it, he used the wind to catch himself, hovering in front of the thing. It's teeth were huge. Kane sliced his hands at the Leviathan's face sending sharp torrents of wind at it. He could see where the wind blades struck the monster's skin, but they had little effect.

The Leviathan swatted at him. It was slow enough for him to maneuver around easily. Kane continued attacking its face. *If I can't hurt it, the least I can do is slow it down to give the others more time.*

Ash continued striking the Leviathan with a barrage of lightning attacks from atop Raimir's back. He could see the thick hide of the beast crackling, small fissures beginning to appear. If he had several days, perhaps then he would be able to fell the monster by himself; however, Ash knew he didn't have that kind of time. It was nearly to the beach now.

On the waters below, Ash could see arrows, spears and javelins, and balls of fire being flung at the creature. He could see Kane fluttering around the Leviathan's face and attacking with slashing movements. It was thwarting the beast, but not enough. It would reach Asmaria.

Then it did.

The titan marched onto the beach with the ships closely following. The warriors moored the ships and quickly dismounted, continuing their attacks. The earth mages were finally able to be of better help. They did everything they could, short of sinking the entire island themselves. Spikes of dirt and rock erected from the ground beneath the creature's massive feet. This caused the Leviathan to roar in anger and pain, but did little else.

Allow me to try something. Hold on tight, Raimir ordered. Ash squeezed with his legs and gripped as tight as he could the feathers of the black bird. Raimir flew in close, just in front of the Leviathan's face. It opened its mouth as if to eat them, but at the same time, Raimir pulled his wings back as if he was going to flap them hard. Ash felt the bird summon a great deal of energy and, with a forward flap, blue lightning erupted from the tips of his wings.

The bolts entered the beast's mouth and Ash saw blood fly from inside. The Leviathan loosed an ear-rupturing screech at that, and Ash knew what needed to happen. However, all of this seemed to make the thing more invigorated to destroy their home. It's footsteps quickened and then—much to Ash's horror—it was stomping on trees. Then buildings.

They flew around its head, trying to strike the inside of its mouth again, but it seemed reluctant to open up for them.

I have an idea, Ash transmitted. *Fly close to the top of his head.*

When Raimir acted in kind, Ash leaped from his back and landed on the monster's rough head. It felt like a reptilian rock, if that was at all possible. Then he waited. He sat in a crouch with his Atlantean bow poised in hand, three arrows of amethyst nocked in its string, and waited for the creature to open wide again. Then a streak of orange and gold in the sky caught his eye.

Clash of Powers

Gethin came soaring in atop Vesta's scaly dragon back, a javelin of light held steadily in her hand. She hurled it at the beast, piercing its chest. The creature thrashed wildly, almost causing Ash to lose his balance. The Leviathan clawed at the wound that was now spurting blood.

Then it continued trashing Asmaria under its feet. Stomping, swinging its monumental, clawed hands at the buildings below it. Nothing was safe. The mages continued an onslaught of an attack; the monster had wounds littering its entire body but showed no sign of dying.

"It's face!" Ash screamed as loudly as he could at Gethin as she made another pass by. Their eyes connected and he could see that she understood. As she came back around, Vesta's mouth opened and her tongue curled. Ash saw the black of her throat become red, then orange, and then a spout of flame exploded into the monster's eyes.

It roared.

Ash sprang from the Leviathan's head, diving like an Olympian. He pulled back on the string of his bow, summoning as much magical energy as possible. He could feel it amping up within the arrows. He was upside down, passing in front of the open maw of the creature. As he released all three electrified arrows, he knew his aim would be true.

He watched as if in slow motion; his arrows went inside the creature's mouth, followed by a second javelin of light. The two magics met in the beast's throat and exploded with a force that nearly created a shockwave. Ash continued to plumet as the Leviathan took three large drunken steps backward into the ocean.

Raimir was suddenly beneath Ash, creating a soft landing for him. Ash turned to look and as the Leviathan crashed into the sea, cheers of triumph met his ears. He looked below and found nothing but pumping fists from his fellow Asmarians.

The destruction was devastating. Nearly every building, house, or hut was obliterated by the Leviathan. The Asmarians would have no shelter to stay in for the next couple of days. The mountains remained intact, keeping the dragons and other critters that lived there safe, but that was mostly it.

Luckily, Avani had the bright idea to construct several shelters out of rock and soil. The Atlanteans gathered along the shoreline with the Asmarians—those who weren't killed in the attack—and talked merrily amongst each other. Most were just thankful to be alive.

It was agreed that a new burial ceremony was to take place for their dead comrades. Since Gethin was no longer in the Tree state, there was no use in offering their bodies to her. So pyres were formed and the dead Asmarians left the world as ashes.

Ash sat in silence with his closest friends. And Augustus.

"You should have seen him," Quinn boasted in regard to Borg. "He was chucking spears like it was nothing! And then,

I saw him catch two of our friends by the backs of their shirts as they were being thrown overboard!"

"Yeah, he's a crafty little devil," Kane commented. The goblin slugged him on the arm and everyone laughed.

While they sat with a fire flickering between them, a wind mage by the name of Niko came up and said, "Just spreading the news; the Guardians and Lady Gethin are in agreement that we leave tomorrow."

"Tomorrow," Quinn repeated. "I didn't think it would be so fast."

"Why?" Ash asked. "There's no point in staying here and waiting for Aros and his army to finish us off. Might as well try to catch him with the element of surprise."

"I guess that's true."

Kane cleared his throat. "Now seems like a good time to tell us what you got up to during those weeks in the other world." He looked at Ash hopefully.

Ash glared back. "It was weeks for all of you, but for me, months." After the collective gasp, he said, "Time moves faster there." And then he dove into his tale.

The Great Battle Begins

sh sat upon the back of his black-feathered friend; Kane, Quinn, and Kailani were on the ships below. The Guardians flew in front of the formation on the backs of the Asmarian dragons. Augustus and Rick were below as well, as were all the able-bodied fighters from the island, whether they be mage or not.

The battle would be upon them soon enough, and Ash couldn't help but ponder how things would be when it was all over. Raimir was flying smoothly enough that Ash was able to meditate as King Dolgatha had shown him. Legs crossed, eyes closed, arms resting on his knees with palms facing the sky.

He thought about Gethin and her declaration that she would die in order to defeat the demon king. Ash hoped she was wrong, but she hadn't been thus far. The powerful being of light magic sat at the foremost ship with Quinn and Kailani. Their closer bond hadn't gone unnoticed by Ash.

The night prior, they'd all learned of what had become of each other in the period away from one another. Ash found himself extremely proud of his friends. The two girls had found the Sword of Pescalon, defeated its protector, and smote one of the demon king's sons. Hearing about the Princes of Darkness hadn't come as much of a shock to him.

Ash had also listened intently to Kane's retelling of his time in the enemy's camp. He developed a new respect for his white-haired friend. What he'd done couldn't have been easy. Ash couldn't fathom torturing another human—even if it was Augustus—just to prove his loyalty. To live among the myriad of monsters in the encampment must have been terrifying as well.

Ash recalled everything he'd learned in Tuvetal and steeled himself to die. It scared him, he could admit that to himself, if not to anyone else. However, no matter how scared he felt, he was even more prepared to do anything to win this fight, even give his own life.

Before leaving Tuvetal he remembered Dolgatha telling him, "Many warriors believe themselves brave enough to withstand battle. To put their lives on the line for the greater good. They will believe they are more prepared, stronger, resilient, than they really are. This is why you must be *certain* of your abilities. Believing is good, yes, but *knowing* is far better."

We draw close, Raimir said. *I can feel it, like a cacophony of snarls and evil voices.* His mental voice seemed to shudder within Ash's skull. He'd never heard him sound like that.

We have to win, no matter what, Ash transmitted.

Agreed.

Ash could see them surrounding an ebony tower that jutted from the ground. Hundreds of wicked beasts in various sizes. He knew the numbers, as did all that were about to lay siege to the enemy. He knew they would be outnumbered, but outclassed? No. He knew for a fact that his comrades were better in every way than the horde of filth.

The ships landed and the warriors crawled off like ants about to swarm a dead animal. They were followed by the Atlanteans King Gabriel could spare; many left behind to rebuild Atlantis. Ash could see the hulking frame of Thaoc from the air, his size only paling in comparison to the giants of Aros' army. Raimir circled around and landed just behind the Guardians. The dragons stayed put for the moment and Raimir stopped next to Iguru. Ash climbed down and walked behind the Guardians who waltzed closer to the awaiting army with Gethin at their side. Her being there seemed to invigorate the Asmarians. Ash glanced around, taking note of the steely looks of determination on most of their faces.

Aros materialized from the shadow of a giant that stood at the peak of the enemy. The sight of it all reminded Ash of the face off that armies of old would enact back when cannons and muskets were popular.

Aros was wearing what looked like white slacks, white dress shoes, and a white dress shirt and vest. It was a ridiculous outfit for what was about to happen. Ash thought that perhaps he wanted everyone to see the blood he planned to cover himself in. A chill ran along his arms.

Appearing to the left and right, slightly behind him were the remaining two demon sons of his. Aros stretched his arms wide and his voice roared, "Welcome, my friends." That's when something occurred to Ash.

All the tents and huts had been removed from the battlefield as if they'd never been there. The only thing that looked the same as Kane described was the tower. It's almost like they knew they were coming and the element of surprise they thought they had, wasn't there at all. Ash turned and found

Kane, their eyes met. It would seem Kane noticed the same thing.

Ash sprinted up to the Guardians and tapped Avani on the shoulder. Without looking, the man said, "What?"

"They knew we were coming," he said, loud enough for the others to hear.

Apparently it had been loud enough for Aros to hear as well, despite them being at least 50 meters apart. "Of course I knew you were coming," he yelled to them. "I knew you would be coming as soon as I sent that white-haired brat of yours away."

"Sent?" Bora scoffed. "He escaped!"

Aros chuckled, "Oh? Did he? Are you sure I didn't allow him to run off with the narrative I wanted?" He laughed wickedly. "Do you *really* think I'd rely on something like the moon blocking the sun for a few minutes to kill all of you?" He let the question hang in the air.

Some of the fear Ash used to feel at every turn was etching its way back into him. Raimir must have felt it too. *Steady. You can do this, Ash.*

The reassurance definitely helped calm him.

"I hate to be the bearer of bad news," Aros drawled. "Well, not really. But you have traveled all this way just to die. I knew you would come a day or two before the eclipse. I knew you would bring the sword with the goal of destroying my obelisk. I hate to tell you this, but you will never get anywhere close to it."

"We will," Gethin argued. "And with its destruction, you will die."

"We shall see." Aros grinned. Then, chaos erupted as Aros uttered, barely audible to Ash, "Kill them all." His army melted around him like a river of venom. Monsters swarmed forward.

Ash decided not to wait for anything; he bolted for Raimir. As he climbed on the bird's back, he heard Gethin and the Guardians scream in unison, "Attack!"

The command was met by the sound of a few hundred warriors surging forward with the cry, "FOR ASMARIA!"

Chasing Shadows

The storm of war thundered in the atmosphere. Death was almost immediate. Whether the first blood belonged to the Asmarians or the demon king's ilk, Kane wasn't sure. He had launched himself immediately, rage and adrenaline surging within him. This scale of war he'd never seen, or imagined. His wind was like having a giant invisible hand, flinging enemies as far as possible.

When the white-haired mage landed, his karambits flew to his hands and he was a whirl of blade and flesh, cutting down ghouls and trolls. The blades didn't seem to do as much against the giants. Their skin was too thick. The wraiths that stood in front of him met the same fate as the others. They were quick but Kane was quicker.

"To the Guardians!" Kane shouted over his shoulder. The mages who heard him answered his call. Augustus flanked his right, Borg on the left. A glance over his shoulder showed Rick closing in as well. They pushed through the horde, obliterating enemies. When they reached the Guardians and Gethin, the group was completely surrounded.

Kane wasn't sure they needed help at all though; the squad of five was thrashing the enemy combatants left and right.

A sword made of light flashed as Gethin struck down three ghouls with one swipe of the blade. Then he saw her: Kailani. She was moving through enemies slowly, slicing through muscle and bone with her chakram. Each time she threw the round blade, she'd recall it before a monster could strike.

Quinn fought alongside her. The Sword of Pescalon gleamed as she hefted it through the air. How she was lifting it, he didn't know. His attention snapped back to Kailani.

"Ah!" she cried out in pain as a giant's club clipped her leg. She took a fall, grimacing and clutching her knee.

A roar ripped from his throat, almost primal. He called on every bit of magic he had. His hands lifted towards the sky as thunderclouds were forming. He used them to his advantage, bringing them to the ground.

A funnel appeared, wind spinning over 100 miles per hour. He swept his hands across the battlefield and the tornado that he controlled picked up and launched every enemy near Kailani and Quinn. The energy it took left Kane on the ground and breathing hard.

"Borg," he gasped. The goblin knelt beside him and placed a hand on his back. "Get Kailani back to the ship. Please." Borg nodded and dashed away. After picking her up, Quinn retreated within the circle of mages that had formed around the Guardians.

"Get that sword to the tower," he told Rick and Augustus as they helped him up.

"You got it," Rick said. The two men trotted forward as Kane retreated.

Ash had been striking down monsters with his bow and electrified arrows. He saw Thaoc and Gabriel tearing through the dark army, trident and war hammer striking them down easily. Then he saw Aros killing Asmarians as if they were nothing. It filled him with rage. *I need a bit of time,* he told Raimir.

He sat on the bird's back and closed his eyes, concentrating on the world around him. His mind poked around in the atmosphere above the battle and he used the magic within him to pull clouds, knitting them together. He could feel the lightning forming inside them.

When he opened his eyes he saw that Kane had conjured a tornado from them and wiped out at least fifty of the horde. His eyebrows shot up at the sight of it.

Then he jumped from Raimir's back, telling the bird to watch over them. He fell until seconds from impact and he called on the lightning from the sky. As it arced past him, he grabbed it, hitching a ride; Ash landed on the ground just as he did when he returned to Asmaria. He looked up, purple crawling over his entire body like a shroud of lightning. Aros was standing with his back to Ash, holding an Asmarian in the air by one hand. A knife of shadow stabbed into the fellow soldier.

Ash lashed out, lightning pouring from his hands. The demon king spun about, blocking the attack with the dead Asmarian's body. He shut off the current of lightning. Aros smiled at him and then vanished within the tumultuous battle. The two Princes of Darkness appeared in his place with nasty grins.

"Ready to die, boy?" one of them asked. Ash barely heard it over the clanging of metal.

Ash offered no response, and instead, whipped his bow out with a snap. Two arrows of lightning were nocked and sent flying at them within a seconds Each arrow clipped the respective brothers in the shoulder. They howled as the bolts drove into their sickly flesh.

The lightning mage used their pain as a distraction, and charged. He just wanted to pound on something. Ash focused his magic into his fists. He jumped and swung down hard at the demon on the right. His fist of lightning connected with the demon's jaw and made a sickening crunch. He spat black blood.

A kick to his back let Ash know that the other demon had recovered. Ash whipped around and the brothers each had stygian daggers in their hands. The boy smiled, standing up straight. He saw something they didn't.

His smile confused them; the brothers looked at each other. One asked, "Why does he smile?"

"Someone is behind you," Ash answered. As they turned, their heads were met with the mighty war hammer of Thaoc. "Thanks!" Ash yelled before dashing back into the fray of bodies.

"Anytime, kid!" he heard the giant man yell.

Ash found Aros again, this time waiting on the boy. His arms were stretched to the sides, slightly bent at the elbows. A dome of darkness was enclosing around him. His grin sent a flash of rage through Ash.

As Ash walked forward, his way was blocked by a giant. The thing had seemingly come out of nowhere. It raised a massive, spiked club in the air, but before he could swing it down, Ash reached toward the sky and yanked down. A natural bolt of purple lightning streaked to the ground in an instant. The giant was dead before his body fell.

Ash saw Augustus and Rick both run into the dome of

obsidian. "No!" he shouted, but they had already crossed into it. The boy ran as fast as he could towards the dome.

Atonement

Quinn was pushing forward with the Bane of Darkness swinging madly at any creature foolish enough to get within reach. The swift blade cut through the monsters like a hot knife through butter. She was within a circle that was formed by her comrades. Kailani was injured and carried away only minutes before.

The girl could see the dark tower getting closer. The giants were becoming thicker the closer they got to it. Seems like Aros didn't want them getting inside, which makes sense seeing as that's where the obelisk is supposed to be.

Watching Gethin smite down their foes with her light magic was mesmerizing. Quinn almost got grabbed by a ghoul a time or two because she found herself gawking at the performance.

Gethin was dual wielding curved blades made of light and slashing through the demon king's ilk with ferocity. The stench of dead creatures filled Quinn's nose and made her want to gag.

A wraith dashed in through the protective circle from Quinn's right. The girl swung the blade and missed. A spike protruding from the bright-eyed creature's wrist was inches from penetrating her neck when she was suddenly skewered by a trident. Quinn smiled knowingly.

"Thank you, King Gabriel," she said as he retrieved his weapon. He gave her a smile and a nod, his eyes wild. He must be enjoying this. Then he was off, back into the throng.

A dome of pitch black arose several meters away, drawing Quinn's attention. She saw lightning rip from the sky and obliterate the giant standing there. *Good luck, Ash,* she thought.

As Ash stepped into the dome, every bit of sound on the outside was drowned out completely. Rick and Augustus were already clashing with the demon king. Aros had a look on his face of boredom as his tentacles of obsidian blocked and nullified nearly every attack.

Augustus had fists of fire that he was trying to strike with. Rick wielded a sword and shield. Ash found himself glad his father was there; it would be impossible to see without his flames.

Just as Ash was about to spring into action, someone—or something—jumped onto his back, snarling in his ear. Its breath was putrid as it tried to gnaw on Ash's neck. He kept his eyes on the fight in front of him as he reached over his head.

Augustus transformed a flame into a sword, lunging at Aros. His blade was met by a stygian scythe and then Aros kicked him in the chest, knocking him to the ground.

Ash grabbed the creature on his back and hurled him over his head. It was a goblin. The creature bared its jagged teeth at Ash and lunged. Ash focused magic into his entire arm, encasing the fist. He met the goblin with one of the hardest punches he'd ever thrown. Blood ejected from the goblin's mouth. The goblin fell to the ground, dead.

Ash looked back up as Rick was being tethered to the ground, a tendril of shadow snaking around each of his legs. He hacked at them tirelessly, but it was futile. Augustus was fighting at a tendril that was wrapped around his neck. Aros strolled forward with a cocky air about him. The scythe was raised above his head. Ash was frozen, unable to move as the blade dropped towards Rick.

The obsidian blade entered flesh with a loud squelch. Blood speckled the ground. Though, it did not belong to Rick. Somehow, Augustus had torn free of his binding and thrown himself in front of the scythe at the last possible second. Aros cast him aside, a look of annoyance on his face as if the fire mage had ruined his fun.

Augustus looked over at Ash who had wide eyes; he smiled and blood dribbled down his chin. Rick stared at the man who just saved his life.

With a growl and a roar, Ash sounded more animal than human. He reached to the sky and called down a torrent of lightning. The amethyst rockets peppered the dome, piercing through and eating away at it. He heard Aros laughing before disappearing as the sounds of raging battle returned. Ash and his two fathers were encased in a protective barrier of lightning that acted like impenetrable pillars.

The boy continued to rage, although he no longer had to pull the lightning from the sky. He merely kept it going with the willpower of his mind, and the ire within.

Ash fell into the mud next to Augustus, the flames on his hands dying out. His breathing was ragged. "No, stay with me!" Ash shouted.

Augustus had a faraway look in his eyes. "I'm… sorry… for everything," he uttered through wet breaths. Blood soaked his sternum.

"Don't you dare leave me! Not again!" Ash felt Rick's hand on his shoulder.

Augustus smiled sadly, a tear crawling down his cheek. "I hope… I have atoned… for my… sins."

Ash smiled at him as the tears began to fall from his eyes as well. "Of course you have. Just stop talking. You're going to be okay. I'm going to get you out of here."

Ash turned to Rick. "We have to help him!" Rick shook his head solemnly. There was nothing they could do.

Augustus' breathing sounded painful then. He was trying to hold on. Ash knew what he needed to say, even though he didn't want to say it. "It's okay. You can let go." He looked the man in the eyes. "I'll be okay. Go be with mom, Dad." And that was it. The fire mage's breathing ceased and the light faded. Ash reached out and closed his father's eyelids with a shaky hand.

Rick pulled him in tight when he stood to his feet. "I'm sorry, son," Rick told him.

Ash let go, forcing himself to pull it together. He took several deep breaths and ended the barrage of lightning strikes. He would have to wait to mourn. Monsters began to pour in around them. Ash and Rick went back to slaying as many as they could, all the while Ash kept looking for Aros.

Jasper was more frightened than he'd ever been before, but he would not relent. He would not back down from this fight. He followed closely to the group protecting Quinn. Jasper wasn't incredibly gifted with weapons, but his earth wielding wasn't bad. Each monster that stepped in his way was met with a chunk of rock to the face.

Jasper found that ending the lives of dark, vile creatures was fairly easy. He didn't feel sick at the thought of killing unless he imagined another person. Lucky for him, none of his current enemies were people. Of course, the ghouls once were, but not anymore. The young mage was pelting a group of trolls baring down on him when suddenly, all of his allies dropped to the ground.

Looking around, Jasper realized they were almost to the base of the black tower. The trolls were also looking around in confusion. Then, at the top step of the tower, just before the door stood a woman. She was leaned forward and looked to be screaming. Naturally, Jasper couldn't hear anything. He could feel the vibrations in his chest though.

This is it, he thought. *This is my moment, my opportunity to be like Kane, Quinn, and Ash. My heroes.*

The vile hands of goblins and ghouls were nearly upon him when he decided to act. All around, Asmarians were being punished for having hearing. The crushing weight of responsibility was on his shoulders as Jasper realized it was all up to him.

The young mage bolted toward the screaming lady, calling on all the confidence he could muster. He felt his magic swirl within himself as he conjured the ground to rise beneath his feet.

Quinn's ears felt as if they were bleeding. She clutched the sides of her head and screamed as all her comrades were doing, although, nothing but the wail of the banshee could be heard. Then, a boy appeared. An earth mage flying through the air. No, not flying, she realized. He was conjuring pillars of rock to his feet with each step, running up them as if it was a staircase.

All around them, Asmarians—both mage and not—were being struck down. For a reason beyond her understanding, this scream didn't affect the enemy. Then, sorrow hit Quinn like an arrow to the heart. A giant brought its spiked club down with vehemence.

The club landed on the back of its target. A man who was bent over, grasping his ears. His body flattened against the ground, and he tried to rise again. The giant slammed the club down again. Then a third time. Three blows is what it took. Thaoc—the gentle giant of an Atlantean—had perished.

The boy reached the banshee, jumping to the top step where she stood, and shoved her. The banshee rolled down the steps and landed on the ground. The creature's torturous wailing stopped and the Asmarians recovered.

Quinn was then able to surge forward, glancing at the boy as she passed him. "Thank you," she said. He only nodded in return.

A knot cinched in her throat, choking her. She wanted to scream, to cry. Any death of an ally was harrowing, but to lose Thaoc was unthinkable. She *had* to destroy the obelisk. Finally, she was in the tower.

The Fall of a Giant

He saw it happen; his large, lumbering friend was killed. It couldn't be real. He had to be imagining it. How could Thaoc die so easily? No. He admonished himself for thinking like that. Thaoc went out like a true warrior, a hero. Ash saw the smaller Asmarian crawl out from beneath the larger Atlantean. He'd shielding her with his body. The anger intensified; Ash was not about to lose anyone else that was close to him.

Ash found Aros trying to flee to his tower. He couldn't allow that; moments before he saw Quinn enter with the Sword of Pescalon. She was so close to destroying the obelisk and only needed time. Ash steeled himself to do something that would wear his body down. Possibly so much that he would be unable to hold himself up, much less continue to fight.

He crouched slightly, focusing his magic in his legs and feet, feeding the muscles, renewing their strength. He blasted off, sprinting past Aros at the speed of lightning. Ash stopped just short of the first stair leading up to the tower. His legs trembled from exhaustion as he turned around to face the demon king.

Finally, Ash thought. *That cocky smile is gone.*

"You die now," Ash taunted.

"You cannot defeat me," Aros laughed. "not entirely. I am *immortal,* you fool! I will just take over some poor bastard's mind later on. It may be a thousand years, but I will win in the end. When little piss ants like you are no more!"

"That's where you're wrong. See, we've discovered how it is that you lived the last time Gethin fought you." At the sound of her name, Gethin appeared at Ash's side, smiling triumphantly.

"Look around you, Aros," she said, gesturing to the fading sounds of battle. Ash hadn't noticed it dwindling either. "Your compatriots diminish even now. Soon, all of your army will be decimated, as will you."

"So, you plan to gang up on me, is that it?" Aros had wide, fearful eyes. "Too afraid to face me one-on-one?"

"No, actually," Ash commented. He made a promise to Gethin that he would do his best to see that she wasted as little energy on the demon king as possible. Ash planned to make good on that promise, especially now that his father and Thaoc were both gone. He wanted to end the slimy demon more than anything.

The mage walked forward, willing his legs to be strong, but he'd used too much energy. They wobbled. Gethin reached out and steadied him by the shoulders. Her hands glowed softly and he felt a renewed vigor spread within his body. His legs felt steady. He smiled at her thankfully, and marched on.

"You've caused me, my family, and my people far too much pain," he said, imbuing his words with as much menace and confidence as possible. "In Asmaria, we have trials to ascertain one's guilt for wrongdoings. Aros, I find you guilty, and now, you must die."

Aros laughed, "Very well. Let's see if you can follow me up here." Aros sprouted black wings of shadow and jumped, flapping the wings to gain altitude.

The inside of the tower is basically how Kane had described it. Quinn made her way through the first chamber and found the spiral stairs on the far end. Up and up she sprinted, breathing hard. Finally reaching the top step, she flung the door open hard.

A squad of ten goblins surrounded the throne and the obelisk. The statuesque structure itself was a regal sight to behold. Runes that shone a dark blue riddled the surface. The goblins slowly stalked forward as Quinn stepped into the room.

I've made it this far. No sense in failing now.

She sprang to the nearest goblin, lashing out with the Bane of Darkness. They were all thrown off guard and the first goblin died. The others attacked swiftly. Small knives and claws came from every direction, shredding her clothes and the flesh of her arms and legs. The little creatures would attack, retreat, then attack again.

Quinn began blocking and parrying, taking out two more goblins before the sword was knocked from her hands. The goblins dived for the blade.

Quinn noticed her folly; she'd momentarily forgotten that she was a water mage. Water flowed from her hands, the Atlantean tattoo shining as she froze the water. Goblins slipped left and right.

The water mage exploded around the room, slicing through the creatures with daggers made of ice. There were only two remaining when she retrieved the Sword of Pescalon.

Before Ash could respond, a blur of white crashed into the demon king. Bora on the back of the white dragon, Kolora. The dragon thrashed at the wings on the demon's back, shredding them apart. He fell to the ground. Upon landing, however, he began moving his hands in intricate patterns, growling as he did so. Shadows formed and twisted, then took on a shape.

In a matter of seconds, he'd crafted a wyvern that was far larger than Kolora. He breathed life into the shadowy beast and it sprang into the air. Gethin threw a javelin of light at the black dragon, hitting its tail. A wound appeared, seeping shadow, but the dragon did not slow. It was on Kolora and the Guardian almost instantly. Ash lunged after Aros, the screams of the dragon filling the sky.

Aros had his back to Ash as the boy sprinted toward him with a bolt of purple in his right hand. That's when an explosion rocked the top of the dark tower sending large black stones raining down on them. Ash formed the picture of a full body shield in his mind, conjured it with magic, and then covered himself. The debris glanced off his lightning shield.

He glanced up, "Quinn!" he shouted, fear rippling through him again.

Not her. I can't lose her too.

Then he saw Kane propelling himself upward and that gave him a bit of relief. If she was still alive, Kane would help her.

Choking sounds caught his attention. Ash turned back. Aros was staring at his hands. His mouth was agape and it looked like he was struggling to breathe. Shadows from the sky snagged Ash's eyes. The other three Guardians were flying to aid their fellow Guardian. Ash could hear the agonizing screams of the white dragon.

"If you're going to do it, now's the time," Gethin said behind him. "If you find it too difficult, I will slay him."

"No, I promised I would. And I do it gladly." Aros appeared to have recovered a bit, but Ash had turned to face Gethin, and didn't notice. He only saw her eyes widen as Aros lunged. She tried to pull him away but wasn't fast enough.

A rod of obsidian plunged through Ash's stomach, causing him to inhale sharply. The pain was immediate and intense, but he'd trained for pain. Without wasting another moment, Ash conjured a bolt into his hand and thrust it into his own stomach. The searing pain almost made him cry out as he drove the bolt through himself and into Aros. The amethyst bolt struck the demon right where a heart would be.

The shadowy rod vanished and the pain increased as blood spilled from the wound. Ash let go of his magic and fell to the ground. He looked behind him as he sat on hands and knees; Aros lay in a pile, twitching in his death.

The demon grunted, and shadows trickled from his mouth in dark wisps. "I'll... be right back," he choked out with a wry grin.

Ash rolled to a sitting posture and turned his head to Gethin. "Unlikely," was all he could say.

"It's time," Gethin said, kneeling beside Ash. She pulled his head onto her chest and he accepted the embrace gratefully.

"What do you suppose death is like?" he asked. Gethin had been closer to death and recovered than anyone he knew. He could feel himself getting sleepy. The agony in his abdomen was annoying. "I think death will feel like when Rick would carry me to my bed after I fell asleep on the couch."

Gethin smiled down at him with bleary eyes. "You will be alright, Ash." He doubted that.

"How do you know?"

"I will make sure." She smiled, noticing Ash's confusion. "I saved you once before when I was the Tree."

He nodded. "I remember."

"There is one last thing I can do for our people," she said as a dagger with bright gold and white hues formed in her palm. "Or I guess two last things." She chuckled.

Ash was sad, but things could have gone worse. He didn't want to see her go, to say goodbye so soon. However, he knew it had to be this way. Not everyone gets a happy ending. Not even the heroes. Too many of them had met their end that day.

"Do not mourn me for long," Gethin said. "I'd rather you celebrate the life I've lived, for it has been a good one with many adventures. You will tell my story, won't you?"

Ash still couldn't understand why she was telling him this. He felt he would be right there with her in the afterlife if there was one.

"Of course," he told her, grinning. His eyebrows knit together. But won't I be seeing you soon?"

"Not quite," she said, smiling all the while. Then she drove the dagger into her heart, inhaling sharply as golden ichor flowed over her hands. She let go of Ash, slumping against him then. He tried to hold her up, but slipped to the soft ground. He groaned with pain.

Ash could see her face, her eyes. The brightness faded and what remained was irises of a deep green hue.

Gethin's body disintegrated, bursting in a shower of sparks like millions of fireflies. The glittery gold flecks meandered into the sky and imbedded themselves into the clouds. Those clouds that Ash had conjured with magic. Golden rain began to fall over the battlefield, but rather than water, it was a strengthening light that soaked into their skin. When Ash looked at Aros' body, he too had disintegrated. All that remained were the flakes of ashen residue floating away.

Healing Rain

The light that rained down upon the Asmarians washed over them, healing their wounds. It was like a light of salvation. Ash slowly climbed to his feet, moving his hands all over his stomach and chest. The wounds had completely knit themselves back together. The golden light still sparkled all around, and it went on that way for several minutes.

Ash could see what remained of Aros' army either fleeing or dying as the Asmarians finished them off. Most had chosen to flee at seeing their leader turned to dust. He'd been defeated.

"Thank you," Ash said, looking up at the clouds. One last note of gratitude to Gethin.

Ash began to make his way to the tower. As he was about to walk in, Quinn walked out with her arm draped over Kane's shoulders. "Are you okay?" he asked her as she fell onto him.

"She used her water to ice magic to save herself from the explosion," Kane answered. "Took me a minute to get her out from under all the rubble."

"I'm okay," she said with a nod. Ash took her from Kane, hugging her tightly. When they broke apart, she grabbed Ash by the face and planted her lips on his.

Kane chuckled as heat flushed Ash's cheeks. Quinn laughed and said, "I should have done that a long time ago."

The befuddlement he felt was replaced by dread as he saw the Guardians walking away from the battlefield. Avani was carrying something, no, someone. Leena stopped, breaking down in wails of despair. He saw the white garb of the wind Guardian in Avani's arms. Bora was dead.

He glanced around the tower; off in the distance, three dragons huddled around one other that lie motionless on the ground. Kolora too had been killed. Aros was gone, but Ash wished he could come back just for a moment so that he may inflict the pain of a thousand deaths upon him.

Ash and his friends were huddled together on one of the ships making its way back to Asmaria. All ten ships were returning, but three of them carried their dead. Ash was thankful to not be on any of those. As they sat there, the weight of everything lifted from them and they all cried silently. They were only kids. Kids that had been thrusted into a war at too young an age, and there were others younger than they who'd been there too.

Ash would never forget the sacrifice many of his people made that day. He wasn't much of a writer, but he vowed to ensure the story of what happened would never die. He would make sure the Asmarians who fell were remembered for generations to come.

As the battle had waned, Borg apparently convinced the remaining goblins to lay down their weapons. He was leading them back to their caves as their clan master. It had been a long time since goblins had manned the great goblin city of Imnin.

Back on the island, the Guardians would have a mass funeral ceremony for all their dead. The rebuilding of their island would begin in the days ahead. Ash and Rick decided they would travel for a while. They would leave shortly after the ceremony. There were others who planned to leave Asmaria behind as well, at least for a little while. Many of the warriors—brave as they may be—would have mental scars from what happened that day. The wounds of the mind could last a lifetime.

The ceremony was fraught with tears and cries of anguish, as well as shouts of joy and laughter as everyone recalled good memories of their comrades. Ash wasn't sure which of the fallen he cried harder for. He was glad to have Quinn's hand in his, crying right there alongside him.

"I'll see you when we get back," Ash told Quinn as he hugged her. He couldn't believe she had finally kissed him and he was already leaving her. He wanted her to come with them, but she felt her duty laid with restoring the island.

She had tried to get him to stay just for the night; there was a party to ensue the following morning. They were to recognize one hero in particular. The boy who had saved their army from the banshee. Without his brave actions, who knows what would have happened? When he told her no, that he wouldn't be staying, she said, "Well, I'll be waiting for you."

Rick and Ash were off and away into the big blue sky. Raimir carried them for the last time to their destination. "You deserve a break from everything," Rick had said. "After all you've done for the Asmarians."

"You did just as much as I did," Ash said.

"I don't think that's very true." They laughed, sitting together on Raimir's back. Ash thought about how he would never feel those feathers beneath him after they arrive to their destination.

The skyscrapers of New York rose in the distance, growing as they got closer. It looked so foreign to him now. Raimir landed and the two dismounted.

It has been my honor to fight at your side, Ash.

Likewise. Ash dared not speak more in fear of losing control of his emotions. He'd shed so many tears lately. Already he could feel a knot in his throat and heat rising in his eyes. He'd cried so much recently that he was tired of it. He hugged the bird's neck, squeezing tightly.

If ever your world finds itself in danger again, Raimir began, *I may find myself as your companion once more.*

Ash laughed, *Let's just hope it doesn't come to that.*

Then he was gone. Raimir flew into the sky and vanished in a flash of lightning and a reverberating crack of thunder.

The two walked through Birkwood Park, breathing in the fresh air and listening to the symphony of birds. Rick pointed to the bench where he'd found Ash as the wriggling bundle of joy. They looked at it for a while. "So, where do you want to go first?" Rick asked.

Ash, the boy born on a lightning bolt, destined to save the world or be its doom. He had certainly saved it, but not alone. He could never have done it alone. "I don't know, somewhere tropical maybe?" Laughter was the loudest sound in Birkwood Park.

Epilogue

One Year Later

As Ash and Rick climbed off the boat onto the great Island of Asmaria, Ash couldn't help but think about when he'd first arrived there all those years ago on the back of a giant bird named Reginald. They were met with open arms and wide smiles. Ash felt he looked relatively the same as he had a year ago, although Kane told him he'd gotten taller.

"I'm liking the new outfit," Ash said, marveling at Kane's wind Guardian clothes.

"Awesome, right?" Then he looked down. "Of course, I would have preferred Bora to not have died." The other Guardians hadn't arrived in time to save her or Kolora, but Aros had paid the toll for the lives he took.

"That goes without saying," Ash said. "But it was your dream. I'm sure she's proud of you. Youngest Guardian in history!" Kane smiled and they hugged again.

"It's good to see you, but I have to get back," Kane told him, flying off to take care of Guardian business.

Quinn led them to the temple that had been erected for their fallen warriors. They walked through the building, hand in hand. Ash paused and read every name on the walls. Some of them he knew, some he didn't.

Bora.

Thaoc.

Augustus. Ash was glad they'd included him, despite his past grievances. He lingered on that name longer than the others.

There were many, many more and he would never be able to thank them all enough. Rick went and found some things to do by himself while Ash and Quinn walked the island.

"Just like old times," Ash noted.

"Huh?"

"You showed me around back then, when I first got here."

"Oh, yeah. I did. What do you think happens next for us?" Her voice took on a more serious tone with the last sentence.

He had to think about that one, as if he hadn't thought about it already. He wasn't sure what was in store for the Asmarians. One thing he was certain of was that if another threat to humanity ever arose, the Asmarians would be there to protect the world.

About the Author

DC Sumner goes by many titles. Some of them include Christian, husband, father, and now, writer. Mr. Sumner serves as a Unit Training Manager in the US Air Force and hopes to be a best-selling author one day.

Besides reading and writing, some of his hobbies are hanging out with his family, watching The Office on repeat, and practicing Brazilian Jiu-Jitsu. DC loves to make new friends and meet new people. One of his biggest hopes for this writing journey is to inspire others to follow their dreams.

You can connect with me on:
- https://dcsumner.com
- https://is.gd/qkC1u1